SMASH
AND
GRAB

PETER CLAWSON

Copyright © Peter Clawson 2024.

All rights reserved. No part of this publication may be reproduced, stored in a retrieval system, or transmitted in any form or by any means, electronic, mechanical, photocopying, recording or otherwise, without the prior permission in writing of the publisher, except in the case of brief quotations embodied in a book review.

CREDITS:
Jonathan Kerry
Phil Kerry

Contents

CHAPTER 1 1

CHAPTER 2 13

CHAPTER 3 20

CHAPTER 4 28

CHAPTER 5 35

CHAPTER 6 43

CHAPTER 7 51

CHAPTER 8 59

CHAPTER 9 66

CHAPTER 10 72

CHAPTER 11 79

CHAPTER 12 85

CHAPTER 13 93

CHAPTER 14 100

EPILOGUE 109

CHAPTER 1

Strange things can happen to men left unattended in supermarket car parks while their girl-friends do the shopping, but Robert Shaw was totally unprepared for the sudden appearance in his rear-view mirror of a naked girl pursued by what appeared to be a Nubian slave wielding a gigantic scimitar. He was even more shocked when the girl raced up to his superb Jaguar XJ220, flung open the passenger door and hurled herself inside, almost falling on top of him.

'Get the hell outa here!' she gasped. 'He'll cut us to pieces!'

Up to this point Robert had been a perfectly respectable citizen with sound prospects and a pleasant if somewhat strait-laced fiancée who believed in sex only after matrimony; in fact the sort of safe middle class British background that nude women in fear of their lives did not fit into at all. So it is hardly surprising that his stunned brain refused to give any instructions to his inactive limbs.

Fortunately the girl had no such inhibitions. Self-preservation was all that mattered to her at that moment.

'For heaven's sake, drive!' she yelled, shaking him in a manner that was altogether too provocative to ignore. Robert gaped, his mouth opened and closed but words failed him.

'Drive!' she screamed.

Robert remained frozen.

'Oh, my God!'

In fact God did nothing. It took an almighty crash which shook the car with considerable violence to bring him out of it. The girl had already opened the door again and was half out when he slammed it into gear and gunned it forward, glancing in his mirror to see the Nubian raising the scimitar high above his head to bury it once more deep into the Jaguar's previously immaculate boot. Things happened in quick succession; the girl slammed the car door, the Jaguar shot forward and the scimitar swung down missing it by inches and sending up a shower of sparks as it hit the concrete surface of the car park. Robert swerved to the left and then to the right, as he hurtled out of the precinct, cannoning off several other vehicles in the process, and by the time they had reached the street, his beautiful car was no longer as sleek and graceful looking as it had been when he took delivery just a week previously.

'Move it!' the girl screamed. 'He's got a souped up super truck!'

Panic drove him out into the fast lane, on past the Ice Stadium, round and along London Road, where a succession of traffic lights each turned to red at the wrong moment and hindered their progress. Robert kept looking into his mirror, dreading pursuit, but there was a solid wall of vehicles as far as the eye could see. Once over Trent Bridge and out of the worst of the rush, he relaxed a little and eventually pulled into a lay-by near the canal.

'Right, you're safe now. Out you get,' he told the girl, who looked at him disbelievingly.

'What, like this?'

'Like what?'

'Nude! Naked! Starkers! Whatever you call it in suburbia.'

This further outburst angered Robert, who by now had almost regained his composure and hated more than anything to be called suburban.

'Look Miss, Ms, Madam or whatever you like to call yourself, I have never seen you before, I didn't invite you into my car. Had it not been for your lunatic friend back there, you wouldn't have been here now and I wouldn't be wondering what the hell my fiancée is going to say when she finds out what happened. So please get out before I throw you out.'

The girl smiled, leaned over and gave him a kiss on the cheek.

'I'm sorry. I did take a diabolical liberty. But what could I do? If you hadn't come to my rescue, he would have killed me.' She tried to snuggle up closer and sighed: 'My hero.'

But Robert would have none of it.

CHAPTER 1

'Out! Or I shall come round, open the door and drag you out myself.'

The girl grinned again.

'Oh my, you're so masterful. But I wonder what **they** would make of that?' She indicated an approaching police car.

'Keep down!' hissed Robert. 'They might see you.'

But the girl took no notice. She simply opened the passenger door and stuck out one shapely unclad leg as if she were going to alight in full view as the police drove by. Robert panicked, flung open his door, jumped out and ran round to the other side, trying to bundle her back in. The reaction of the police was predictable. With sudden realisation that all was not as morally right as it should be, they did a screeching handbrake turn and headed back towards the halted Jaguar. The girl's reaction was equally quick. She threw herself over into the driving seat and sent the car into turbo-drive, leaving Robert stranded by the roadside, the police in two minds what to do and passers-by agape with astonishment.

The police car drew up with a screech of brakes beside Robert who was gasping and pointing, too many words trying to come out of his mouth at the same time.

'She … she … stole … my car! They already chopped it up and now she's stolen it … stop her!'

The police driver discarded his colleague and then shot off in pursuit of the girl. The constable came over and tried to calm Robert down. There was a park bench on the canal bank and he ushered him over to it.

'There now, sir. You sit here and I'll take a few notes about what happened.'

'Happened? You saw what happened. She stole my car!'

'Yes, but there must have been a reason. You were together in it until then … and pardon my asking, sir, but am I right in thinking the young lady wasn't wearing any clothes?'

'What? Oh, yes. That's right. I'd never seen her before in my life.'

The constable's expression became long suffering and officious.

'I see. I wonder if you would mind blowing into this plastic bag, sir?'

Being such an upstanding citizen, Robert had never been breathalysed before and at first he failed to catch on.

'I see. We're not refusing to take a breathalyser test, are we? Because that would be a very serious offence, sir.'

Robert was just about to tell him where to stuff his breathalyser when there was yet another screech of brakes as the Jaguar – his Jaguar – hurtled to a halt next to them.

The girl opened the passenger door and yelled: 'Quick! I lost 'em! Get in!'

Totally confused, the policeman just stood there, unable to take his eyes off her.

'Don't worry, Constable. It's quite an eyeful, but you soon get used to it after a while. Best thing is to cool off while you can.'

So saying, Robert gave the officer a hefty shove, which sent him tottering to the edge of the canal, grasping helplessly at thin air, and eventually toppling into the stagnant waterway. The water was only waist deep, but it was enough to delay pursuit long enough for Robert to vault the bench and dive into the car as the girl put her foot down again. They disappeared as the policeman scrambled out of the canal and ran into the road, frantically trying to blow his whistle and flag down a passing pursuit vehicle. Turning round, Robert had a glimpse of the police car retrieving its hapless former occupant as they swerved round a corner, slowed to a respectable pace and then swung into someone's yard, where the girl stopped the engine and ordered him to get down so he couldn't be seen. Seconds later the police car swept by, siren roaring, lights blazing, quite oblivious to their hiding place. They gave it time to fade away into the distance and then burst into torrents of laughter, which also faded quickly when the house-owner appeared at his door and started walking towards them.

'Time to go, I'd say,' the girl ventured. 'Shall I drive or will you?'

'You can,' said Robert. 'By the looks of him, the sooner we're out of here the better.'

So to the man's amazement, they drove out of his yard without a word and headed off in the opposite direction to the police as if nothing had happened. The man went back into his house muttering: 'Naked … smooth as a baby's bottom … well I'll be …'

'What?' asked his wife.

'Nothing,' he replied. 'She was, though. Blest if she wasn't.'

Back on the road the atmosphere in the Jaguar was relaxed again.

'Well,' said the girl.

'Well what?'

'Well it's difficult to throw the driver out, so where do you want to go?'

'I don't know.' Robert shifted uncomfortably in his seat. 'Somewhere discreet, with no police and no maniacs.'

'Somewhere discreet, with me dressed like this?'

'Undressed!'

'Does it matter?' she sighed.

'It does to me.'

'So what do we do?'

'You could do the decent thing.'

'Such as?'

'Stop the car and get out.'

'Or we could go to your place.'

One thing about this girl, she could make the most ridiculous suggestions seem the most sensible in the world, thought Robert.

'Oh yes. I can just see it now, old Mrs Gardener suffering another stroke, her husband threatening to report me to the police again and Fanny Palmer waiting by the gate, all night if necessary, to tell Grace about the "naked trollop" I brought home. Yes, we could go to my place, if you wanted to ruin my life as well as my car.'

'I could wait in the car while you went in and fetched me some clothes.'

'They would be too big for you – oh, take the next left, then turn right at the end of the street – my clothes I mean.'

The girl took her eyes off the road long enough to give him a wry, knowing look.

'Not yours … hers. She does keep some there?'

Robert fell neatly into the trap.

'Yes … I mean … how dare you make such personal suggestions. Besides, I don't think Grace would approve if I allowed someone else to wear her clothes.'

'Right, so that's settled. We'll park in the drive; you fetch me a coat or something and Bob's your uncle. Which way now?'

'Right. It's number 10, set back off the road … Hell! What am I saying? No, we can't. It's impossible.'

But as the girl so rightly pointed out, anything is possible, anything at all. Without another word she drove sedately into this driveway and motioned for him to do as she had said. Robert hesitated, shrugged his shoulders and said: 'What the hell! It's too late now anyway. One thing though. If you are coming into my house the least you can do is to tell me your name. After what we've been through I think I deserve that much.'

The girl smiled warmly.

'Hella,' she said.

'Yes,' he replied. 'I suppose it had to be.'

Obviously impressed with his luxury Spanish ranch style home, Hella made herself as inconspicuous as possible.

'Go on then,' she urged. 'Make a respectable woman of me.'

But Robert continued to hesitate. Across the street a curtain was moved: only a fraction of an inch but it was enough.

'Damn her,' he cursed. 'Old Groucho Gardener is on the alert. She'll have her beady eyes trained on us from now on.'

'Surely she can't read anything into you getting out of your car and going into your own home,' said Hella.

'True, but it's when I come out again and take you inside that worries me.'

'Hella pouted.

'Listen. I'm the one who should be worried; going naked and defenceless into the home of a man I only met today.'

'The day you're defenceless, I'll fly to the moon,' he laughed. 'And I'm scared of heights.'

Nevertheless he plucked up the courage to leave the car and enter the house. Hella watched him go with a strange smile on her face. Ordinarily she had little time for men, except when they could be useful to her or for pleasures she had no desire to get from women. But this one was different. Somehow he had got under her skin and she didn't know for sure whether she liked the feeling or hated it. Glancing up at the window across the street, she caught a glimpse of old Groucho as Robert called her, before the curtain flapped back into place again. What she didn't notice was the beaten old pick-up truck which cruised slowly past the end of the drive before Robert returned with his coat.

'There you are,' he said. 'It's the best I can do. I hope it fits.'

Struggling into it before getting out of the car, Hella glanced up at Mrs. Gardener's window again and smiled deceptively. Then with deliberate audacity she turned to face those prying eyes and flung the coat open wide like a flasher's mac in a public park. The effect was startling, for the curtains swung to again, but this time it was as though someone behind them had been taken so much by surprise that they had fallen off their seat, grabbing the drapes as they did so and pulling them down. A face appeared at window sill level, eyes blazing, and Mrs. Groucho mouthed the single word 'Hussy!'

Luckily for Hella, her host was so intent on getting them both safely and discreetly into the house that he failed to notice the incident.

'Come on,' he called. 'If anyone sees you we're done for.'

'I think we're done for then,' Hella laughed.

Air conditioning made the interior temperature just right, even though late afternoon sunshine was beginning to give way to a cooler evening and Hella was about to discard the coat when she remembered her nakedness underneath.

'I don't suppose Grace leaves any dresses here by any chance?'

'Why should she do that?'

'Oh, I don't know. Just a thought. No offence meant. Perhaps I could borrow one of your shirts. They make ideal mini-dresses.'

Robert fished one out of the linen basket.

'Here. It's not ironed I'm afraid but it will have to do.'

'Grace only does the ironing once a week, I suppose.'

After pouring two neat whiskies, he went and sat beside her on the grey toned sofa.

'How d'you know I liked the "low flying bird"?' Hella wanted to know.

'It wasn't difficult.'

'Does Grace like a drop of the hard stuff?'

'Enough about my fiancée for now. Let's talk about you, shall we?'

Hella smiled wickedly.

'That's what I like to hear. Come closer.'

But Robert was having none of it, for the present.

'Not until I get some answers, especially as to how you came to be naked in a supermarket car park, chased by a maniac with a scimitar.'

'It's a long story.'

'I expected as much.'

'I could shorten it.'

'Just so long as it's the truth.'

As she settled more comfortably into the soft cushions, pulling the shirt bottom almost down to cover her knees, he couldn't help noticing the expression in her lovely eyes. Hella could turn reality into fantasy with eyes like that and he wasn't sure how long he could hold out against such a highly sensual assault.

'We had been together for about two years when I discovered he was a conman with a prison record, and when I tried to leave him he said if he couldn't have me, no-one else could.'

'You expect me to believe that?'

'I don't care what you believe,' she replied, reaching over and pulling him into her arms, those beautiful eyes threatening to drown him in sensuality.

'But I'm a respectable businessman with a suspicious fiancée,' he protested. 'Yes, wait a minute. I didn't check the answer phone. Maybe she left a message.'

Both relieved and frustrated that he had managed to escape for the moment, Robert moved back so quickly that his passionate guest almost fell on the floor. He went over and switched on the answer phone.

'I must ask you to treat everything you hear with strictest confidence,' he told her, though the words sounded ridiculous then.

'Of course,' chuckled Hella. 'Soul of discretion me.'

The machine issued a series of bleeps, electronic noises and static before clicking into gear to reveal that there had been a call from Grace and an ominous one at that.

'Robert!'

There was more clicking, a stifled cry from Grace and the line went dead. A loud metallic clang of coins dropping into the box at the other end heralded her return.

'This is Grace, remember? you left me at the supermarket. How could you? I'm on my way now, by taxi. I hope you have a good explanation.'

The line went dead again and he suddenly realised the enormity of his problem. If grace found Hella there, in her present state … He shuddered at the very thought. Hella regarded him intently.

'Not good eh?'

'Bloody diabolical, actually!'

'What are we going to do?'

'I am going to sit here and wait for Grace. You are going to do that coat up and leave this house immediately.'

Hella couldn't believe it.

'What, like this?'

'It's decent. What more do you want?'

'Old Groucho across the road will love it. The gossip will last for days. It might even reach your beloved Grace. In fact, if Mrs Gardener has anything to do with it I'm sure she'll be the first to break the news about your unwelcome visitor.'

'Can't be helped.'

'Oh yes it can!'

Before he could stop her, she had moved across and undone his trousers, which fell to his knees. He was still fumbling with them and trying to prevent her from removing any more of his clothing when here was a terrific explosion out the back. They both froze.

'What the hell is that!' he cried, stumbling towards the kitchen as he tried to pull up his trousers again. He might have made it but for the fact that Hella grabbed his arm just in time.

'What are you doing?'

'I've had enough of this he gasped, trying to break free of her. 'I'm going to find out what this is all about.'

Before he could utter another word, however, there was another explosion and the door to the kitchen blew out. Had Robert been near it at the time, he could have been killed. Fortunately the shock caught him off balance and Hella was able to drag him away into the hall and to the stairs.

'Quick!' she hissed. 'He'll need time to reload. Upstairs!'

Robert's brain scrambled again. His thoughts came out incoherent and illogical.

'But Grace! He'll kill her!'

'Have you thought it might be Grace?' Hella chuckled. 'Hell hath no fury like a woman scorned, you know.'

She continued to drag him, protesting, up the stairs as the sound of pursuit came from the lounge below. Another tremendous explosion rocked them.

'Whoops! There goes the telly!' she cried.

As Robert tripped, tottered at the top of the stairs and nearly crashed down them, she somehow managed to haul him to safety and they tumbled into a bedroom, landing in a heap on a magnificently upholstered double bed. Almost immediately he started scrambling to remove his trousers, but Hella was neither enticed nor amused.

'You must be joking! We're being hunted down by a homicidal maniac with a 12-bore shotgun and you want sex?'

'Not sex,' panted Robert. 'A swim.'

Tumbling off the bed, he ran across to the big double windows and flung them open.

'I always take an early morning dip, so we had the pool built directly under the bedroom window. Come and see.'

It took Hella two seconds to follow him, but just two more to gasp: 'I'm not jumping down there!'

However, another shotgun blast from the stairs which blistered the bedroom door changed her mind. Robert threw his trousers down by the side of the pool and dived after them, hitting the water with perfect precision. Hella teetered for an instant, then as the bedroom door bust open, she also flung herself off the balcony, hitting the water with a loud scream and an almighty splash. Winded, she doggy-paddled after Robert who executed a superb front crawl to the side of the pool, hauling himself out and dragging her after him. The slight lull in pursuit from upstairs must have been for reloading the shotgun, for as they ran over the lawn to the garage, their attacker appeared at the window, took aim and blasted off both barrels again. In the garage it was obvious the damaged Jaguar was going nowhere. Its tyres had been slashed to ribbons and the front bonnet stove in.

'Now what?' Hella demanded.

'Prepare to die …' he began, but then stopped. 'Wait a minute. See those keys on the wall? They belong to Grace's Fiesta. It's parked outside on the street. She always leaves it there while we go shopping.'

'But how are we going to get to it?'

'Easy. We go through into next-door's garden, along the side of the hedge and he won't be able to see us.'

Their departure was echoed by the sound of another shotgun blast and more valuable breakages in the house, but for the moment all they wanted to do was to escape with their lives. There would be plenty of time to plan a counter-attack later.

'Are you sure he's just lovesick?' Robert asked as they drove away in the designer Ford Fiesta. 'The way he's acting, you would think he'd lost his family jewels.'

Hella cuddled up closer to him.

'I told you, he's crazy about me. I am his family jewel. Don't I have the same effect on you?'

'Right now the effect you have on me is sheer terror. If the maniac doesn't kill me because of my innocent association with you, then Grace will.'

'Well, if that's the case, let's pull over and at least give them good cause.'

'Not until I've put enough miles between us to make it safe.'

'Which is where?'

'A small motel I know not far from the airport. Even Grace doesn't know it, so we will be able to relax for a while and sort out what to do next.'

She was still clinging tightly to him as they sped along the dual carriageway out of the city, but by this time she was sound asleep.

CHAPTER 2

When they arrived at the Midway Motel, so-called because it was situated on the A52 halfway between Nottingham and Derby, Robert had great difficulty extracting Hella from the car. She was sleeping so soundly she simply refused to wake up.

First he tried to pull her up by her arms, but she didn't budge. Then he tried to swing her legs out, but each time he did so they flopped back inside again. Hella was obviously just as stubborn when asleep as when awake. In the end the only thing left was to put his arms around her shoulders and try to haul her out. But before he could even attempt what for him would have been an impossible task, the little vixen flung her arms around him and hauled him into the car on top of her. In the process he banged both knees on the sharp metal of the door frame and let out a yelp of pain.

'You little bitch …!' he cried in uncharacteristic fury, but was then silenced by another firm hand grasping his shoulder and a stern voice in his ear.

'Excuse me sir. Is there anything wrong? Can I be of assistance?'

The new side of Robert, brought out by his unbelievable encounter with the most wilful little brat he had ever met, wanted to tell the car park attendant where to go. But the image of Grace's stern but striking features glaring in his mind stifled his words. He was in enough trouble as it was, but his feeble attempt to explain made things worse, especially when Hella suddenly burst back to life.

'It's my daughter,' he gasped. 'I can't seem to get her out of the car.'

Before the bewildered jobs-worth could reply, Hella dragged him further down on top of her.

'Oh Daddy!' she cried and kissed him so passionately on the lips that his senses swam. The trouble was, he was just beginning to enjoy it when the yellow-jacket cut in again.

'Here! Steady on! There's no need for that. Let me help.'

So saying he pushed Robert aside, cradled her naked thighs with his huge gnarled hands and hoisted her legs out of the car and held onto them tightly, signalling Robert to pull her the rest of the way until she was upright.

Hella tried to stage another dramatic collapse, but the two men were too quick for her. Robert kept her shoulders straight while the attendant clasped his arms round her waist and lifted. Obviously this couldn't continue indefinitely but somehow they managed to spin her round so that each of them supported one side of her as they half hauled and half dragged her towards the motel entrance.

'Help!' she yelled, alarming several other guests arriving and departing. Fortunately none of them had the courage or the will to interfere. Hella kicked her legs, squirmed, but finally allowed herself to be bundled through the door and escorted to the reception desk where the manager waited, arms folded and an inscrutable expression on his face. He dismissed the parking attendant, then spoke.

'Mr. Shaw,' he said in the non-committal style used by all good motel managers. 'How nice to see you again; you and your lovely … er … er …'

'Daughter!' Robert chimed in a little too emphatically.

'Ah yes … daughter … So young but so … Do sit down my dear. You look all in.'

Hella gave the man that look Robert knew could melt steel, followed by innocence beyond imagination. She then flopped down into an incredibly comfortable leather upholstered armchair and appeared to fall fast asleep again, having ensured that the coat slipped from her shapely thighs and legs but still protected her innocence.

The manager took all this in without comment but with obvious relish before speaking again.

'Now Mr. Shaw. Despite your somewhat unusual arrival I presume you would like a room for you and your … er … daughter. She will be sharing of course …'

'Yes .. daughter,' Robert faltered, grateful that the manager made it quite clear he understood the overall situation but chose to make no further comment. 'Is my usual free; on the first floor at the back?'

The manager consulted his diary and smiled.

'As it happens it is. The previous guest departed this morning. How long will you be staying?'

'Oh just the weekend. We'll be leaving on Monday morning. Shall I pay now?'

'No. We'll put it on your account.' He indicated Hella. 'The young lady – your daughter – seems to have dropped off. Would you like some help with your bags?'

'No. It's all right. I'll manage with her and we'll fetch our bags later. They're still in the car.'

So saying, Robert leaned over Hella and whispered: 'Come on. Wake up. We need to get to our room.'

He tapped her on the shoulder and the only response was a loud reverberating snore. She was obviously doing this for effect. Robert turned and looked towards reception, shrugging his shoulders helplessly. Then he spun back again, leaned right over her so that no-one else could see what he was up to, reached down and pinched her thigh where it melded into her rump.

This was totally uncharacteristic of the person Robert had been before this whole escapade had started, but now he realised that when your whole world goes haywire the only answer is to float along with it.

His action produced immediate success as Hella shot upwards so suddenly she butted his nose which spouted blood all over her coat – his coat!

'Oh no!' she sobbed. 'I'm so sorry. I didn't mean to do that!'

Fishing in her pocket – his pocket – she pulled out his best handkerchief and dabbed at the flow of red. Robert recoiled, produced another hanky. He held it firmly to his damaged nose while ushering Hella towards the lift. One of the manager's assistants rushed in front of them, pressed the button and stood back to let them in as the door opened. They staggered inside, Robert striving to be brave in spite of the pain and Hella desperately trying to atone for causing the injury.

Once in the room, Robert sat her down on the double bed – double bed. Oh no! Then he dashed into the bathroom. Fortunately the bleeding dried up after half-an-hour of cold water dowsing and several ruined towels. The agony proved to have been caused by severe bruising but no broken bones.

As he returned to the bedroom Robert realised he was still fully dressed. Hella on the other hand, was not. She was flat out on the double bed completely starkers and also sound asleep, his coat discarded in a crumpled heap on the fluffy carpet.

But what disturbed him most was that this did not embarrass him as it would have done before they met. There was also the fact that he had never actually seen this amazing girl properly dressed. For the first time in his well ordered life temptation reared its sexual head but even Hella had not yet broken down all his inbred and Grace induced inhibitions.

'Pull yourself together Robert,' he muttered to himself as he gently put his arms under her lovely body and began to lift her from the bed, intending to draw back the covers. The intention was to put her to bed properly, settle her under the sheets and attend to his own sleeping arrangements up to now undecided.

Good intentions, however, can often lead to disaster and before he could set himself Hella's arms snaked round his neck. Seconds later he was lying astride her on the bed. Horrified, Robert tried to extricate himself, but her grip was too strong.

'For goodness sake!' he gasped. 'Let go.'

If anything she pulled him even closer. As his senses spun in all directions, he realised in further horror that his unpredictable companion was in fact still fast asleep. What on earth was she dreaming?

'No! Don't go there. Don't even think about it,' he told himself.

The alternative was, of course, to do what he had intended all along. It took an almost super human effort to regain his footing, haul her into an awkward fireman's lift and complete the job. When at last it was done and she was comfortably settled down, he realised that against all the odds, Hella was still lost somewhere in her dreams fast asleep!

By this time Robert was so confused in mind and emotions he hadn't realised his own predicament. Here he was, a previously respectable member of the community, cohabiting a motel room with a naked girl he had just put into a double bed; the only place for him to sleep being with her.

Oh! To hell with it! He flung off his clothes except for his trunks and slipped in as quietly as possible beside her. Fortunately the only reaction from Hella was an impatient grunt, but mercifully she didn't wake up.

The next thing Robert knew was that he woke up in the early hours after a nightmare in which Grace was screaming at him like a raving lunatic. The very thought of what she would do in light of what had gone on during the course of yesterday, terrified him more than the dream.

Then it hit him! His mobile! She was bound to have left a message. Very carefully he eased himself out of bed, picked up his discarded jacket and took the phone out of the pocket. Dare he switch it on? He had to and Grace's angry voice blurted into his ear.

'Robert! What on earth is going on? Have you gone stark staring mad? Where's my car? If you've damaged it. This place looks as if a bomb has been dropped on it! I can't believe it. And that girl. Some of the neighbours say she was naked. Honestly! I shall never be able to show my face round here again. As for you, they're getting a petition up to have you evicted, what with three of the older ladies being found totally distressed by your antics. Please tell me it's all a bad dream. There's even talk of having you certified, Robert! Get in touch with me immediately and bring my car back safe and sound or I shall never speak to you again!'

With a click the message went dead. As dead as he would be when Grace caught up with him. Unable to think straight he slumped back onto the bed, only to be disturbed by a violent shaking again. This time it was not a dream, but in all likelihood another real nightmare beginning to unfold.

'Wake up! Wake up!' Now it was Hella shaking him like a rag doll. 'Look at the window! The lights! Flashing! Sirens! Listen!'

Robert tried to get his head together rousing himself onto one elbow. Almost falling back. But then he caught sight of the curtains. There was no doubt about it. The beams were headlamps; the blue and red flashers police emergency lights.

A second after seeing them, he was over the room peeping through the curtains. As the car came to a halt the lights were dowsed, the noise abated and two policemen got out in that lazy way they do when trying to look nonchalant. A drawl in motion someone once said. Casually they strolled towards Grace's Fiesta, giving it a once-over with their powerful police torches before heading towards the motel's main entrance. They had almost reached it when another wave of even stronger headlight beams swept into the car park followed by a roaring Demolition Derby rig.

'Oh no!' cried Hella. 'Not that. Please don't.'

'What the hell is going on?' Robert demanded. 'Who is that and what are they doing?'

'You know who it is but you don't want to know what he's going to do!' she sobbed.

Outside the DD rig huffed and puffed like a bull about to go on the rampage. Lights flashing, funnel fuming, the driver backed a yard before roaring across the car park between the police vehicle and the Fiesta, completed a skidding handbrake turn, before hurtling back towards Grace's cute little Fiesta, tyres screaming, engine howling and speed increasing more quickly than a dragster. An instant before the collision its front wheels lifted off the ground creating a grotesque wheelie effect and smashing the tiny car's bonnet to pieces. Not content with that, the lorry then drove right over the top of the frail Ford flattening it completely. Just to finish the job, the driver reversed over it again and then wrecked the tiny vehicle beyond repair.

Another handbrake skid which demolished a top of the range BMW and the raging bull was ready to charge again. Revving and roaring; screeching its tyres, straining on the brakes. Smoke puttered out of the exhaust as time and motion was poised for another run.

'Oh my God!' Robert yelled. 'He wouldn't!'

'He bloody-well would!' cried Hella. 'Just you watch him!'

The unfortunate police duo clearly agreed with her, but it was too late even though they raced back towards their car.

Another back kick, swerving charge which sent the officers sprawling out of the way and the rig roared up, smashed down and flattened the police car as it had done the Fiesta. All that came from the wrecked vehicle was the dying wail of a siren somehow triggered off by the crushing impact.

As the two highly embarrassed officers scrambled to their feet and staggered towards the motel entrance, the rig headed out onto the open road and stormed off in the direction of Derby.

'Oh hell!' Robert blubbered. 'That's done it. We're dead meat!'

'Yeh,' Hella agreed. 'They'll throw the book at us.'

But it wasn't the police Robert was worried about. 'Not the law,' he sighed. 'A much more deadly authority.'

'Your fiancée,' said Hella.

'Grace!' groaned Robert.

Before they could utter another word, there was another squeal of brakes and screech of tyres from outside. They both spun round together and looked out of the window in time to see the motel pick-up truck pause long enough for the policemen to climb aboard before racing off in pursuit of the DD rig.

'See,' sighed Hella, only partly relieved. 'First threat didn't materialise.'

'Yes,' came the reply. 'But a much bigger one's on the horizon.'

CHAPTER 3

Twenty minutes later Hella emerged from the bathroom. She had showered and washed her hair which was wrapped up in a makeshift turban. A towel wound around her naked body and tucked in at the top under her arms made her look incredibly seductive.

But Robert didn't notice. He was bent over trying to squint through the wide-angle spy hole in the door.

'What the hell are you up to now?' she demanded. 'Not becoming a peeping Tom are you?'

Without taking his eye away from the peep hole, Robert stuck his left hand out behind him shaking it furiously.

'Ssssh! She'll hear you!'

The expression on Hella's face was incredulous. A picture of mixed emotions.

'You are! I knew there was more to you than meets the eye!'

She burst out laughing.

'The eye!' she cried. 'Get it? I've noticed the way you look at me sometimes – all the time!'

This brought an instant reaction from Robert. Wrenching his gaze away from the peep hole he shouted. 'Will you shut up? She'll hear every word you say. Then what will happen?'

Back he went to his spy glass only to recoil with shock at the sight of a magnified eye squinting through the lens at him.

Shaking himself in a spasm of embarrassment, he straightened up and then bent down again, gingerly peering out. This time what he saw was the backside of a sexy wiggle disappearing through the door opposite which gently closed in its wake.

Suddenly another shock in realisation of what had been missing, Robert shot upright, spun round and stared at his gorgeous companion.

'Merciful heavens!' he gasped. 'What's happening to me? I'm losing my grip!' Then to himself: 'Pull yourself together man!'

Hella simply stood there, posed like a glamour model, chest thrust forwards and her right thigh exposed by the slipping away of the towel's folds. The look in her eye and provocative pouting lips were so strong that no man had been able to resist them before.

So she was not too surprised when Robert muttered an obscenity, shook himself and rushed across the room towards her. After all every man had his level of resistance, even him.

But even so she was totally stunned when he flew right past her, snatched his top coat off the hanger in the open wardrobe and flung it round her shoulders so violently that she nearly toppled over onto the floor.

After regaining her balance Hella stood stock still building up a head of steam. For one ludicrous moment Robert envisaged smoke coming out of her nose and ears, but what emerged from her mouth was much more unsettling. Shaking with fury she hissed through gritted teeth: 'Right! That's it! Never before. Never before has anyone … Now I know what it's like to be a woman scorned and you know what that means.'

So saying she tore his coat off her shoulders and flung it across the room at him. Then she unwound her turban with such a flourish that her gorgeous blonde hair swirled around her head in the most alluring fashion.

Robert stood aghast as the turban was hurled into his face catching him so much unawares that he got into a hopeless mess trying to unravel it.

By the time he had freed himself the body towel was flying his way with similar results.

Once this one was lying on the carpet next to the turban, Robert looked up at a full frontal of the most beautiful and livid woman he had ever seen!. Not that he had seen many in his all-too sheltered life. They weren't in abundance in upper-middle class suburbia.

'Right!' she cried. 'That's it!'

'W-what do you mean?' Robert choked.

Before he could utter another word she sat herself down on the side of the bed, arms folded, expression set, and added: 'I refuse to budge another inch until you find me some suitable clothes to wear!'

Although Robert thought that nothing could be more suitable than the way she looked now, he actually said nothing.

It was pretty obvious that Hella, being the girl she was, could read his thoughts. If nothing else the look on his face was enough.

'Well?'

'Well what?'

'What are you going to do about it?'

Now it was Robert's turn to lose his cool.

'What I've been trying to do ever since you forced your way into my car – get rid of you!'

As soon as the words slipped out he regretted them. Hella dissolved into floods of tears. Robert tried to comfort her.

'I didn't mean it,' he choked.

'Just get me some clothes and I'll be out of your life forever.'

Desperation fired his reaction. He grabbed her by the shoulders and shook her, losing his famous reserve completely.

'For once in your life will you listen?' he yelled. 'I said that in frustration and I didn't mean it. You've changed my life completely in such a short while that sometimes I don't know where I am or what I'm doing.'

His passion was so sincere it melted Hella's mood.

'Well at least get me the clothes,' she whimpered, calming down considerably.

'I know you won't believe me but that is why I was spying on the girl across the corridor,' Robert explained. 'She's about your size. Maybe she would lend you some.'

Even Hella had to admit it was worth a shot.

'Well go on then. The worst she can do is to say no,' she ordered.

How wrong could she be.

As he crossed the corridor to the door opposite all Robert's misgivings about his ability to deal with his current situation escalated.

He knocked softly at first, but then with more conviction after no immediate response. His gaze fell on the spy glass, reminding him of the giant eye trying to see into his own room. But no way was he going to stoop to such an action.

The lift door at the end of the corridor slid open and a member of staff emerged. Robert began to twitch nervously praying the door would be answered before questions were asked. His fears were groundless however, as the man strode past with merely a polite grunt. Seconds later there was the sound of the lock turning and a security chain fastened. The door inched open to reveal that same eye as before, unmagnified, peering at him surrounded by the part of a lovely face which wasn't hidden by the woodwork. The eye blinked.

'Yes?'

Robert was momentarily struck dumb. Then he stammered: 'C-could I come in and have a word with you? It is important.'

The eye blinked again.

'It depends on your intentions.'

Poor Robert! Caught off-guard again.

'I – I – er – assure you my intentions are honourable.'

'Well no then.'

'B – but …!'

But he needn't have worried. The chain was already being released and the handle turned. The door then swung open to reveal a goddess. That was the only word Robert could think of to describe her. Such a vision shattered his already wavering confidence even more. He just stood there, mouth agape, unable to speak or move.

'Oh! For goodness sake come in,' she laughed. 'I was only joking.'

Although Robert followed orders as usual the vision revealed by the wide-opening of the door knocked him back. The other guest was wearing only a see-through 'Baby Doll' nightdress covered by a full-length opaque negligée! But what made it more like some terrifying American horror film was the long, incredibly sharp looking carving knife she waved him with.

Robert's eyes followed its motion to and fro as if he were some helpless prey mesmerised by a fearsome predator.

The girl laughed again, suddenly realising his concern.

'Oh, the knife,' she chuckled, brandishing it in a mock threat at him. 'You thought … You didn't really did you?'

'I didn't know what to think,' he replied.

Her tone softened again. 'I'm sorry. Hadn't realised I was still holding it.'

'Did you think I might attach you?' Robert felt even more ridiculous now.

'No of course not. Actually I was just chopping up a pomegranate to make me more beautiful.'

'And how would you expect to do that?'

She shook her head condescendingly. 'My, my, you have led a sheltered life. Have you never heard that women from Ancient Egypt right up to date have rubbed pomegranate juice all over their bodies to increase their beauty?'

'No I haven't actually.'

'Well, that's what I do too. Would you like to help?'

'No. I wouldn't. I don't even know your name …'

'Nor I yours. But if it matters my name is Rita. What's yours?'

'It's Robert if you must know; Bob to my close friends.'

By this time Rita had let him in and closed the door.

'Then I shall call you Bob, just to show I would like to be your friend.'

Before he could either agree or protest she went on: 'Oh. One other small matter. You must have knocked on my door for a reason. What is it?'

Even Robert with all his inhibitions had to admit to himself how provocative she was. It would have been incredibly easy to acknowledge the fact, but his tortured brain didn't think like that. Honour demanded no less than the truth.

'I – I – er – need your clothes!' he blurted out.

Amusement curled Rita's lips.

'Do you now?' She sighed. It was a statement as much as a question.

'You're welcome of course, but I don't know how well they would suit you. She indicated the seductive night attire she was wearing.

'How about starting with these? You can help if you like.'

Her first move was to pull the bow free at the top of her negligée which had an immediate effect on Robert. He threw himself forward too late, just failing to grasp the filmy garment as it floated to the floor.

'No!' he cried in desperation, but the temptress took his action the wrong way.

'My, oh my. We are an eager beaver,' she teased. 'You can take the nightie off if you're that keen.'

Her seductive reaction actually produced a recoil from her visitor; like touching a live wire.

'No!' he cried aghast. 'That's not what I meant! Is sex the only thing you women ever think about?'

'Only when we think that's what you men want,' she replied coyly, by which time like Hella when she and Robert first met, Rita was also quite naked.

'Oh no! Here we go again,' Robert muttered.

Rita heard him, just. As she was meant to.

'You did say you wanted my clothes so what did you expect me to think?'

She thought for a second. Then mock realisation flooded her much too attractive features.

'Unless of course, as I said earlier, you want to wear them yourself.'

'Don't be ridiculous! They're not for me. I need them for someone else. And not night clothes – day wear.'

'Ah! I see. You're in a relationship and your – er – partner wants to wear them,' she teased.

'Yes. No!!' Robert realised all of a sudden what he thought she thought. 'Look. All this is getting us nowhere,' he added.

Rita twinkled a smile at him. 'I had noticed,' she told him as he floundered around trying to make sense of the way his life was being tuned upside down. 'Let's start al over again,' she murmured. 'No really. I mean it.'

So it was that Robert told her the whole unbelievable story of his life since being bumped into by Hella.

Rita listened with interest and growing amusement. At the end of it she somehow managed to stop herself from collapsing into laughter.

'That is one incredible tale. So unbelievable that I have to believe it, ' she chortled.

'Will you help me then?' Robert begged.

'Of course I will. How could I do anything else?'

She put the knife away , went to her wardrobe and put on a dressing gown. Then she took down a suitcase from the shelf and started stashing clothes in it. Everything Hella would need to make her smart and more importantly, respectable. Her own clothes she draped on the bed ready to put them on.

'If you take the case across to your – er – girlfriend. Sorry, the girl in your room. She can be putting them on while I do the same with mine.

Robert nodded, grabbing the case by its handle, but fumbling with the catch. Rita moved to assist him, but before she could do so they heard the screeching of tyres outside and the sound of a persistent loud hooter. Both of them rushed to the window. Rita drew the curtains aside just wide enough to peep out. Then she let out a cry of anguish.

'Oh no! It's Jack. He's early! Robert started to ask who Jack was but she beat him to it. 'My husband! If he catches you here, he'll kill you. Get out!'

He started to lift the suitcase, but it fell open spilling all the carefully packed clothes everywhere.

'Never mind about them,' she cried, 'Just get the hell out of here now!'

As Robert flung the door open Rita tried to tidy the place up, but there was no time. She did what she could, muttering to herself. 'He'll kill me too! He bloody well will!'

Out in the corridor Robert just managed to miss colliding with the motel assistant he had seen earlier. Somehow the man held on to a tray containing the remains of some guest's in-room refreshments. But then

Rita raced out, slamming the door behind her and cannoning straight into him. He went flying, the tray slipped out of his hands and the food splattered all over the floor. The impact caused her gown to gape open, giving him a flash of her naked body before Hella opened the door for Robert and Rita to tumble through, slamming it behind them.

For an instant there was utter peace and quiet in the corridor. The assistant sat up trying to clear his head, shaking it frantically. Suddenly realising what he had missed, he launched himself to his feet, snatched the tray off the carpet and stalked along towards the lift leaving the mess to be cleared up by the cleaning staff.

CHAPTER 4

As the staff man reached the lift, however, he was in for another shock. He pressed the button, but nothing happened for a few seconds which seemed like hours. Then the usual whirring and clanking began lasting for another lifetime until with another judder and bang it came to rest on his floor. There was yet another seemingly endless pause before the doors grumbled open. Without warning a dark suited figure exploded out, sent him reeling so that the tray banged loudly against the wall as he nearly toppled over again.

'Ta-dah!' yelled the newcomer, then realised his mistake and added. 'Oh! I'm sorry! I thought you were my wife!'

The only reply was an almost incoherent muttered curse and a great roar of frustration as the beleaguered victim staggered into the lift, jabbed the down button and disappeared from view.

'Ah well,' sighed Jack and charged off along the corridor shouting: 'Rita my darling! Hope you're ready! I'm willing and able!'

He was even more thrilled to find the door to their suite ajar and dashed inside with a loud whoop.

'Ready or not, I'm coming!'

No reply. Was she already in bed waiting for him? His mood began to change when he found the bedroom empty, no sign of her anywhere.

'Rita dearest, this is getting beyond a joke. Where are you?'

Still no sign of her. Jack was not and never had been the most patient of men and suddenly he snapped!

Storming back to the door and flinging it open so hard that it banged back against the wall chipping a chunk of paper out of it, he yelled: 'Where the bloody hell are you? Get back here now or I'll break every bone in your body!'

Across the corridor in the other room Rita began trembling like a leaf in a gale.

'He will you know. He really means it and if he finds me here like this with you we're all in trouble.'

Robert had never been the most violent of men. All he could do for the moment was stand there looking and feeling flustered. Hella, on the other hand, had no such doubts.

'Phone him now Rita. It's the only way.'

'I can't. We left the room in such a hurry I forgot to bring my mobile.'

But Hella was not to be put off so easily. 'Use our room line.'

'No.' Robert came back to life and intervened. 'Use mine and ring your own mobile.'

The two women gave him a puzzled look.

'Less chance of detection,' he said uselessly, handing Rita his phone. She immediately dialled the number and they could hear the muffled ring tone in the other room.

Jack snatched it up, dropped it, cursed and then answered. 'What?'

'It's me,' Rita stammered.

'Where the bloody hell are you?'

'It's a surprise,' she said a little more confidently. 'I promise you'll be amazed.'

But Jack was in no mood for games, especially mind games.

'Just get in this bed quick before I come looking for you.'

'I will. I will. You get in and warm it up for me and I'll be there in a couple of shakes,' Rita said as suggestively as she could.

'Now!' Jack almost screamed, switching off and flinging the mobile across the room. But despite his frustration she knew he would already be tearing off his clothes and diving between the sheets in readiness.

Turning to the other two she urged them to get moving: 'We've got to get out of here fast. He's the most unpredictable man I've ever known. If we're lucky he'll lie there for about ten minutes and then come after us.'

Hella pointed out to her that Jack would take a few minutes to get dressed again.

'Not necessarily,' replied Rita. 'If he's in a bad enough temper he will do anything.'

At this Robert threw his hands in the air and shouted 'Oh no! Not again! I couldn't stand it!'

Both women were at a loss to know what he was talking about.

'What do you mean?' Rita wanted to know.

'What do I mean? I'll tell you what I mean! First my respectable contented existence is shattered by the sudden intrusion of one naked girl. Before I can come to terms with that another one appears to make matters worse. Now you tell me I'm to be chased and possibly assaulted by a naked man! What am I expected to do, jump for joy?'

Unfortunately the girls' hysterical laughter served only to incense him even more.

'Add to all that the fact that I am being pursued by a homicidal maniac, an outraged fiancée and the police no less and what do you expect me to do? Thank the Lord for my uneventful suburban lifestyle?'

Somehow his embarrassing and embarrassed companions managed to stifle their laughter and return to the matters in hand.

'All this is very well,' said Rita. 'But if we don't get a move on your nightmare will materialise sooner than you think.'

'Right,' Hella urged. 'Let's go then.'

Rita checked the spy hole and Robert prepared to follow.

'If it's safe,' said Rita. 'Let's go.'

Nothing untoward happened as they slipped out through the door and headed for the lift, which luckily had stopped at their floor to let out a couple of dark suited business men. The trio rushed through the rapidly closing doors just in time to hear a great roar from down the corridor followed by some cheeky 'Oohs!' and 'Aaahs!' And then an ear-splitting scream of sheer agony. Further muffled cries and sounds of a violent scuffle dwindled as the lift descended.

Rita could hardly contain herself. 'That's Jack,' she chortled. 'What did I tell you?'

Before the others could add anything they hit the ground floor, the doors slid open again and they emerged to yet another shock!

'Oh my goodness,' cried Robert.

"What?' Rita asked.

'Through those doors in reception! It's Grace!'

'Grace?' Rita echoed.

'His fiancée,' cried Hella. 'Oh God!'

'Now what?' Rita again.

'It's that maniac as well. Her boyfriend,' gasped Robert. 'And the police. Now what are we going to do?'

Fortunately they hadn't been noticed yet and before they were all hell broke loose out of another lift on the other side of the foyer. Jack burst onto the scene stark naked and all eyes turned towards him. It was then that he realised his compromising state of undress, frantically trying to mask his embarrassment with inadequate hands. His expression of red hot fury transformed to scarlet blushes as an officious constable headed towards him.

'Quick!' hissed Rita. 'While their attention is diverted. Stop ogling my husband and follow me!'

Robert was about to say how much he deplored her insinuation when Hella grabbed his arm and dragged him after Rita down a passage which eventually led to the kitchen.

Past the restaurant and through the swing doors they hurtled. How anyone avoided being knocked over, trays and all, was anybody's guess. Rita spied the head chef and raced up to him. After a few words passed between them, he nodded albeit reluctantly, and she beckoned her fugitive friends to follow. Everyone seemed to accept this as normal behaviour except one junior helper who got a full frontal as Hella's coat flew open before him. The poor lad flushed as red as Jack had been and fainted away on to the slippery tiled floor. Within seconds the trio were outside., awaiting Rita's next instructions.

'See that van over there.' she pointed out. 'That's ours.'

They looked; looked again, then stared in disbelief. Robert was first to speak . He shook his head several times, ever more violently.

'Not that … not that one … not … '

'That's it. The one with the bi-plane on top,' Rita cut in. Her voice sounded as if it was the most natural thing in the world.

'Oh no!' gasped Hella. 'You're not ..?'

'Barnstormers! Got it in one!' laughed Rita. 'We give demonstrations at air shows and wing-walks for a small fee for those brave enough to have a go. In fact wing-walks are free tonight if you want to try one.'

'I hope you don't take off and land on top of the van,' joked Robert. Or at least he thought he was joking.

'Don't be silly,' laughed Rita. 'We only do that in show flights.'

But before they could reply, she added: 'Anyway if we don't get a move on we might have to. Come on.'

So far there was no sign of activity outside the motel. Problems in reception were obviously still to be sorted out. But it was only a matter of time. As the trio reached the van with its cargo perched precariously on top, Robert had another sudden revelation.

'The key! Your husband will have the van key.'

But Rita only smiled.

'Stop worrying will you?' She turned to Hella. 'I don't know how you manage to put up with him.'

'I don't,' said Hella. 'I hardly know him. Remember?'

'Sorry. I forgot. Anyway we keep a spare one in a small compartment behind the door.' Without another word from anyone she retrieved the key and opened the doors. 'Voilà,' she said. 'Jump in.'

The other two needed no second bidding and Rita slid in behind the wheel. She turned the key. The engine spluttered and died. 'Isn't that what always happens?' she muttered. 'Temperamental bugger, just like Jack.'

Robert didn't answer. He was too busy peering out of the window for signs of any pursuit.

'Shit!' cried Rita as she tried again. 'Shit! Shit! Shit!'

But they all relaxed when it fired on the fifth attempt and she gunned it into action. The van suddenly shot forwards and as they swerved through the car park gate gate onto the main road, Robert managed one more glimpse back at the motel.

'There's plenty happening now. People running about in all directions,' he told them.,

'Anyone following us?' Rita wanted to know.

'Not yet, as far as I can tell.'

CHAPTER 4

'Better put as much distance as possible between us and them,' she said, putting her foot flat on the pedal and hurtling along at a frightening speed. As a result the cargo rattled and strained its moorings to such an extent that he vehicle seemed to be on the verge of plunging out of control.

Ever responsible Robert commented: 'Shouldn't there be some sort of a speed limited on a vehicle like this?'

'What? You want to slow down and let them catch us?' cried Rita.

A few hundred yards along the road she suddenly swung the steering wheel violently to the right and they drove into a narrow country lane.

'Now where are we going?' Hella asked.

'Back to base,' Rita explained. 'The last place they would expect us to go. Well for the moment at least.'

The perilous journey continued at an alarming rate until they arrived at a farmhouse with a large hangar at the back. The van swung into the yard and came to a juddering halt in front of the hangar's main doors. Rita pressed a button on the dashboard and the up-and-over doors opened before them.

'Open Sesame,' joked Hella.

'Ta-dah!' cried Rita and drove inside, thumbing the doors closed behind them.

'It won't take them too long to think of this place,' grumbled Robert.

'Not when we're nowhere else to be found.'

'Long enough to get into some clothes and get away again,' she replied.

'Clothes!' cried Hella. 'I'd almost forgotten what it was like to get into some proper clothes.'

'Not quite as proper as you might think, but they will have to do for now.'

'What do you mean?'

'Follow me and I'll show you.'

They climbed out of the van and Rita led them to a small room at the side of the hangar. Inside she opened a lock and explained: 'As I said, not what you might expect, but better than we have now.' She handed what looked like a scantily clad showgirl's outfit to Hella, sparkling sequins sewn onto a semi-transparent body stocking. Before her friend could protest she said: 'The sequins are positioned in just the right places to preserve your modesty, unlike the coat you are wearing at the moment.'

'What about me?' Robert demanded. 'Despite what has happened to my self-esteem recently I can assure you that I am not prepared to wear a costume like that.'

'Nor would I expect you to,' Rita replied with a twinkle in her eye which Robert didn't notice, but Hella most certainly did. 'I can assure you that no-one, not even your beloved Grace will recognise you in this.'

So saying she took down a much more colourful outfit which would certainly protect his identity and his self-consciousness.

'There's even a mask you can wear with it,' said Rita and both girls fell into paroxysms of mirth. But their idea of an hilarious joke fell on Robert's deaf ears.

'This is absolutely ridiculous,' he cried. 'You can't expect me to wear this. It's a clown's costume. I'd be better off in my own clothes.'

'Not where you're going,' Rita chortled, winking at Hella.

'Where is that?'

'East Midlands Airport.'

'Why would I need a clown costume at the airport?' Surely my own clothes would be much less conspicuous.'

'Less conspicuous, but not half as safe strapped to the wings of our other stunt plane – the Stearman. It's fully reinforced. Come on. We'll use the other car to get there. You can change on the way.'

A look of sheer horror appeared on Robert's face and he shook with a mixture of anger and fear.

'N – now you w – wait a minute,' he stammered. 'No w – way am I going to do a wing-walk in that costume!'

'Oh yes you are!' laughed Rita, in true pantomime tradition.

'Oh no I'm not!' he retorted not realising what he had said.

'Oh yes you are!' cried Hella.

'Oh yes you bloody well are!' gasped Rita, almost overcome with laughter.

CHAPTER 5

So there they were; a most unlikely trio looking more like characters from the film 'Those Magnificent Folk in Their Flying Machines' than fugitives from the law, enraged lovers and who knows who else? Rita in the sexiest pilot's suit Robert had ever seen, skin tight sleek as a seal, plunging neckline – more Catwoman than air ace. Hella clad in a semi-transparent flesh coloured body-stocking with fluffy white feathers and multicoloured sequins sewn strategically to preserve her modesty, which they failed to do with any respectability and Robert. He looked a picture of cute embarrassment in his scarlet and yellow spotted clown's outfit, complete with decorative conical crash helmet.

Somehow Rita managed to stop giggling long enough to convince them of the urgency of the situation. 'No more time for panto,' she cried. 'We really do have to get out of here before they find us!'

'Too late!' Hella gasped, having heard noises outside and moved to peer through the small observation hatch in the massive hangar doors.

'They're already here,' gasped Robert. 'Now what do we do?'

'Like I said. Get a move on,' ordered Rita.

'But how can we?' Robert asked as ever the devil's advocate. 'They're between us and the van.'

'We're not using the van. Much too conspicuous.'

'So how do we escape?' Hella wanted to know.

Rita pointed to one of the darker corners of the hangar where a veritable beast of a vehicle crouched ominously.

The other two were stunned. Robert would almost have swallowed his false teeth if he had any.

'Not that!' he choked. 'That isn't what I think it is, is it? Not a 1930s racing Bentley?'

'Well. Yes and no,' Rita replied, somewhat amused. 'It is a Bentley, but it's been souped-up a bit.'

'Souped-up a bit!' cried Robert. 'You couldn't make one of those monsters even more powerful than it already is!'

'Yes you could and we did! So come on! Let's go.'

Robert began pacing backwards and forwards clearly in some distress. His voice became almost hysterical. 'It's a monster,' he muttered.

'What?' It was Hella's turn now, as she headed towards the car.

'My headmaster had one of those. Kept it in a ramshackle wooden apology for a garage in the far corner of the quad. Every morning at break he would fling open the double doors, leap into his pride and joy and with a noise like an explosion, reverse out at speed scattering boys in all directions. Then he would gun it into forward action and career crazily out of the gate without even bothering to look whether there was anyone else driving by. It was chaos; hooters blaring, tyres screeching, brakes squealing and shouts I would be too embarrassed to repeat in front of ladies. He was a homicidal maniac when he got at the wheel!'

His tirade was interrupted by a loud banging on the hangar doors.

'Open up! We know you're in there,' yelled an officious voice. Open up or we'll break these doors down.'

'Oh yeh! You and who's tank,' laughed Rita trying to shake some sense into Robert, who calmed down fairly quickly.

Hella also showed signs of panic. 'What are we going to do now? Use that thing to smash through the doors and scatter them?'

Rita shook her head. 'Nothing so dramatic, she chuckled. 'We'll escape through the rear doors. Let's hope they haven't had time to get round there yet.' Giving Robert an almighty shove, she added forcefully: 'Get them open now!'

'Won't they be locked?' he asked timidly.

'Not from the inside you idiot! Just do it before it is too late!'

As Robert hurried to open the heavy doors wide enough to get the Bentley through, the two girls scrambled aboard and fired the engine.

Just before the leviathan roared into life Rita complained: 'It's a long time since anyone had the cheek to call me a lady?'

Somehow Robert managed to open the doors. The Bentley charged up to him scaring him half to death.

'Jump in!' cried Rita.

'But there are only two seats.'

'Sit on her bloody knee then!' Rita yelled as Hella unceremoniously hauled the horrified man into the car on top of her and they erupted out of the hangar just missing a rather hesitant police officer who stumbled backwards into a hedge.

'Stop!' he cried leaping to his feet again. 'Stop or I'll have you arrested!'

'I don't think so,' smiled Rita, swerving out onto the open road with Robert still all arms and legs in the air all over Hella. Squeals and grunts, cries of pain, puffing and panting, an odd, 'Ouch!' followed by 'Get your bloody elbow out of my cleavage.' Then Robert: 'How can I with your knee stuck in my groin?'

In the end it was all too much for Rita. She slewed into a lay-by and cried: 'Look! I'm not having any shenanigans going on while I'm driving. Sort yourselves out and be quick about it! You get out Robert! You too Hella! Now you back Robert and you sitting on his knee Hella. Right. Are you comfortable? Then I'll drive on. I don't know what's happening back there, but knowing who's involved it will be chaos.'

Actually she wasn't far wrong. In the crowded car park at the barnstormers headquarters people were running in all directions. To make matters worse there was a sharp shower of rain. Hella's wild man motioned Grace to get into the passenger seat of his Daimler limousine. She hesitated getting drenched as she did so. Her flowery dress clung to her in the most revealing manner and he couldn't take his eyes off her.

'What are you staring at?' she demanded.

'If you don't know, I won't tell you, but if you don't get into the car before you catch your death.'

He jumped into the driving seat, leaned over and pushed the passenger door open. Grace ducked in and he turned the heating up to full.

'We'd better get you dried out,' he explained.

Meanwhile Jack got into the white van with the aircraft on top, tried to make a quick getaway only to reverse into an inappropriately parked police car, fracturing the bonnet. A cop leapt out yelling at him, but Jack slammed his foot down as the unfortunate officer grasped for a hand hold and was dragged through the mud before being dumped face down in a deep puddle. His colleagues revved and revved but a combination of wheel-spin and sliding delayed their departure before they stormed off after the other two vehicles giving chase. The unfortunate officer regained his footing, staggered across to the final vehicle, the motel pick-up.

'I'm commandeering this truck. Drive on,' he coughed, spluttering water over the seat.

'What do you think I'm doing?' came the reply.

It was like a 'Devil take at the Hindmost' cycle race, but in this one the last still remained in the pursuit.

⁓

Well ahead the Bentley continued its charge through the countryside. The motorised motley posse were not yet in sight behind when Rita swung the steering wheel hard to the right and drove into what appeared to be a wooded quarry. Fortunately they had missed the rain and had only a few spots on them.

'Robbers Rocks,' announced Rita. 'Prepare for a hair-raising experience.'

'Isn't that what we've had already?' asked Robert trying to compensate between being heard and not shouting his head off over the noise of the engine.

He soon realised how futile his question was as the journey's thrills level suddenly roared from scary to downright dangerous. The Bentley careered along a rough network of lanes occasionally serving precariously to miss small boulders as they drove deeper and deeper into the abandoned quarry which had been restored to give a sort of forestry hills-and-hollows effect.

'Isn't it great?' cried Rita. 'We used to play here as kids. But now it's used to test rally cars and big off-road vehicles.'

'So how did it get its name?' Hella wanted to know.

CHAPTER 5

'Centuries ago it was a mine for iron and other ores. Deep tunnels were bored into the rock at all angles. Later it was a perfect place for outlaws to hide. Some of the tunnels are large enough to conceal even a lorry.'

'Or a Bentley like this one,' said Robert. 'But surely they would find us eventually.'

'Not where I'm going,' Rita pointed out. 'But first we must confuse our pursuers a little … if they manage to have the wit to find the quarry at all.'

An instant later the Bentley leapt out on the straight track heading back at breakneck speed only to be confronted by the police car coming in the opposite direction. As the two vehicles passed at high speed there was a sudden dawning of realisation in the police car and the driver slammed on the breaks, skidding off the track and narrowly missing a tree as it slid to a halt.

In the other direction Rita did a sudden handbrake turn into the nearest off-lane track.

Further back the police car reversed without warning right into the path of Jack's white van, which crashed into a tree. The bi-plane broke its moorings, toppled off the roof, landing in a broken mess on the van's severely shattered bonnet and steam erupted everywhere.

The police car hurtled after the Bentley narrowly missing the Daimler which had just turned into the quarry, followed by the motel pick-up truck. The Daimler's momentum carried it across the track and down the opposite side lane, while the pick-up lumbered straight up the main road. Halfway along it they narrowly missed the Bentley emerging at speed from the right hand tearing into the trees on their left. Two lanes further back the Daimler somehow avoided a head-on collision with the police car. Back came the Bentley into the right hand woods where it disappeared almost immediately among the bushes and trees.

'Hold on to your hats!' yelled Rita. 'Here we go!'

'I'm not wearing a hat!' gulped Robert.

'Hold on to your head then!' Rita retorted. She bent hers low over the wheel.

'Duck!' screamed Hella burying her head in Robert's shoulder.

'Look out!' he warned.

Seconds later the Bentley crashed into what appeared to be a solid barrier of bushes and shrubs. Hella and Robert shut their eyes and prayed for deliverance. Their prayers were immediately answered as they burst through into a small clearing. The supple branches sprang back into place as though nothing had happened. Within an instant the desperate pleas were silently voiced again as another wall of greenery loomed up before them. Fortunately the result was the same apart from the fact that they found themselves in the yawning mouth of a huge cavern. Again their rear was covered by the supple branches springing back into place. Much to Robert's relief Rita brought the Bentley to a shuddering halt.

'Everybody out,' she ordered.

But Robert, the eternal pessimist, remained seated while Hella climbed down off his knee.

'How can we be sure we're safe? They're bound to find us in the end. They won't just give up and go away.'

Rita put her hand on his shoulder to comfort him. 'Trust me, They won't discover this place.'

'I just hope you're right,' Robert replied. Nevertheless he did get out of the car.

Rita told him: 'Now listen.'

'To what?' asked Hella.

'To that,' Rita explained as there was a tremendous crash from somewhere outside the quarry.

'What on earth was it?' Robert interrupted.

Rita adopted her most condescending expression as she told him: 'That my dear Robert was the sound of Hella's boyfriend's Daimler running out of track as it went over a ridge, flew into the air and shattered its springs as it smashed to the ground flat out.'

'Oh no!' gasped Robert. 'What if Grace was with him?'

'I bet she was. He wouldn't be driving a truck like that,' Hella teased.

Robert was devastated. 'She's probably sitting there trapped in her seat injured. I must go to her.'

But Rita restrained him. Her tone was reassuring but firm. 'You know you can't do that. It could take hours to find her in this place. She would blame you and you would lose her anyway.'

'But we can't just leave her and do nothing. No! I have to go.'

'What about your cell phone?' Hella cut in.

'What about it?'

'You could phone an ambulance. Rita knows where we are.' Hella paused for effect, giving Rita a look which said more than any words could. 'She could pinpoint the crash site for them despite what she says.'

Apparently Robert thought this was a good idea. He reached into his pocket and took the phone out. But before he could call Grace it rang.

'Well, go on. Answer it' Rita ordered.

'What if it's her?'

'Oh! For goodness sake,' snapped Hella. 'Answer it!'

After another pause and against his own better judgement, he gingerly complied, hardly daring to put it too close to his ear.

'Robert! Are you there? If you are, you'd better answer. Now!'

Totally unsure what to do he was about to reply when Rita stood in front of him, finger to her lips, shaking her head vigorously. She was too late. He panicked and gasped in the most timid of voices. 'Hello. Who's there?'

'You know damned well who it is; Answer me!'

'Are – er – are – you all right?'

'Am I all right? Listen. I've been driven round open countryside and into this God-forsaken quarry where we crashed. What do you think?'

'But … are you hurt … physically I mean?'

'Of course I'm not, but this is the second wreck you've caused. I know you know where we are, so get over here now! Or you'll be sorry. My God! Will you be sorry!!'

With that the phone went dead and Robert dissolved into a sense of numb panic. His hand shook as he tried to put the phone away again and he almost dropped it.

Once again they were interrupted by a loud bang outside causing Robert even more agitation. It was followed by another one almost immediately afterwards.

'So what was that?' Hella asked.

Rita gave them another one of her knowing looks as Robert withered even further. 'It's obvious,' she explained. 'You don't drive at high speed around this place, even if you know it as well as I do.'

This brought another plaintive comment from Robert. 'You might have warned us before hurtling about like a maniac. More to the point what are we going to do now?'

'That's easy,' laughed Rita. 'I'm going to high-tail it out of here as fast as the old jalopy will take us.'

'What if they see us?' Robert ever the pessimist moaned in despair.

'They won't,' Rita assured them.

'Why?' Hella queried.

'Because we're using the back way. Come on. Get back in the car and hold on for dear life. It will be the roughest ride so far!'

CHAPTER 6

Sure enough it proved to be just that. The Bentley tore through the large but winding cavern like something from an Indiana Jones movie. Twisting turning, sliding swerving, missing walls of granite on one side and large boulders on the other. Accompanied by and chased by the deafening roar and resounding echo of the motor's massive engine, they ploughed through puddles of mud like a water chute white hot knuckle ride at Goose Fair or some nerve-racking theme park spectacular.

Rita was clearly enjoying every second. Robert cowered as low in the seat as he could and Hella clung to him as if he were the last man on earth.

Each sudden break careering corner and subsequent acceleration threatened to tear Hella from his embrace and hurl her out of the car head first into the jagged underground rocks, but somehow she clung on until they emerged into a brightening countryside. No rain now. Just panic at least as far as Robert was concerned. His eyes were everywhere except on his two companions.

'What now?' Rita demanded, noticing his discomfort.

'Just checking,' he replied rather shakily still unsettled by the crazy drive through the caves. 'They might still be on our tails.'

Rita shook her head. 'I don't think so.'

'Why not? If you knew of the back exit surely your husband did.'

'No chance. I told you this was a childhood haunt. I hadn't even met him then. Maybe it would have been better if I never had,' she muttered to herself rather than anyone else.

But Hella heard her. 'What?' she wanted to know.

'Oh nothing. Just musing about what might have been.'

She might have gone into a more lengthy explanation but they were approaching the main road and Robert was worrying again.

'What's to stop them going round the long way and catching up with us?'

'Two things really,' Rita replied in that long suffering way she had of making people feel stupid. 'First it's miles further. Second, from the sounds of the smashes we heard in the quarry I doubt they currently have a single roadworthy vehicle between them at the moment.'

'But they have police radios and mobile phones. They could alert other police to intercept us.'

Hella agreed with him, but Rita was way ahead of them both.

'Reception from inside to and from outside Robbers Rocks is nil. The only way for them to contact the outside world is to walk to the edge of the quarry and try to make contact from there.'

'But I spoke to Grace,' Robert ventured.

'Yes, but you were inside at the time. She couldn't phone you now.'

So saying she drove out of the country lane onto the main Derby road, speeding up considerably as she did.

This raised further doubts in Robert's mind while Hella also looked confused.

'I thought we were heading for the airport,' she observed catching sight of the signpost.

'We are. But in a roundabout way. I'm trying to put them off the scent.'

Robert blustered in again. 'B – but y – you said …!'

'I know what I said but even you must accept that they'll be after us again eventually. Once they get out of Robbers Rocks and call for assistance. One call and there will be cops clambering all over East Midlands Airport unless we fool them into believing we're going somewhere else.'

'But …. but!'

'No more butting. Just leave it to Auntie Rita; things will work out.'

'Yes. But which way?' Hella mumbled under her breath.

'I heard that,' laughed Rita. 'And I won't let you forget it.'

They were now reaching the outskirts of the city. Fortunately there wasn't a lot of traffic about but a number of pedestrians on the footpath and waiting to cross the road as the lights turned red.

CHAPTER 6

At the edge of the footpath a large bald-headed man who looked to be in his sixties, smartly dressed and confident he stepped onto the crossing as a scantily dressed woman – probably in her twenties – left the central reservation.

Rita rolled the Bentley to a growling halt in the nearside lane and a boy racer in an Astra joined them in the outside lane clearly impatient to get away.

'Quick!' cried Rita to Hella. 'Give him a quick flash of your boobs!'
'What do you mean?'
'Never mind why. Now! Before it's too late!'

Hella immediately struggled to do as she was told and Rita shouted at the top of her voice: 'Hey, you!' Frantically waving her arms she added: 'Yeh, you! You with the polished head and dirty mind!'

The man reached the second lane, faltered and turned his face towards them. Hella thrust her ample bosom forwards in the most suggestive manner. The man's attention was focused on her so intently that he cannoned straight into the younger woman coming the other way. Desperately his hands clutched at her shoulders, neck and then, as she kneed him in the groin, her plunging neckline frantically trying to maintain his balance. Out popped her bouncing breast nearly smothering him as she tumbled on top of him onto the ground.

Unfortunately this was when the lights changed, the boy racer stamped on the accelerator realised at the least instant that he was about to run over the two grapplers and swerved violently to the right and crunched his bonnet against a nearby 'Keep left sign'.

'Great!' Rita yelled, put her own foot down and roared safely past them onto a clear street.

Half a minute further on she gave a long drawn out blast on the horn which caused a couple of pensioners to drop their shopping bags with egg smashing consequences.

On again until she swung the car into a garage with a large workshop at the rear.

'Low on petrol?' Robert queried, naïve as ever.
'Change of vehicle and direction.,' Rita replied.

They drew up outside the large double doors of the workshop and an oily mechanic emerged. Rita leapt out of the crouching Bentley and into the garage man's arms. When they finally broke away from each other she made it quite clear what she really wanted.

'She needs a complete overhaul.' she gasped, indicating the Bentley.

'And you need a courtesy car while we're doing it.'

The way he spoke it was supposed to be a question, but his tone was more like a statement.

'Correct,' Rita answered. 'And a courtesy car would be ideal.'

'When and where do I pick it up this time and what do I tell Jack if he comes looking for you?'

'It will be waiting for you in the parking zone at the East Midlands Airport. The private car park that is. If Jack or anyone else wants to know where we're going it's Manchester Airport.'

'What do you mean by anyone else?'

'Oh, the police, my two friends' partners, one of them a homicidal maniac, a security man from the motel back down the road. People like that,' Rita chuckled, hoping she was winding him up as usual.

Luckily her hopes were fulfilled.

'That's OK then,' he laughed. 'I just face being murdered, arrested, set upon by an irate partner or threatened by a suspicious security guard. Take the silver Nissan parked near the pumps. It's just been filled up and checked over.'

Delighted by his understanding and helpfulness Rita gave him another lingering kiss before beckoning the others to follow her. When Robert hesitated she heaved a long sigh.

'Now what's wrong?'

Robert shrugged his shoulders despondently.

'You'll only say I'm being over-sensitive again, but what about that poor old man?'

'Poor old man,' echoed Hella. 'Dirty old man more like. Did you see the way he ogled my boobs? I thought his eyes would pop out of his head!'

Rita joined in again clearly adamant she had done the right thing.

'I checked in my mirror,' she said. 'And from the way he was groping that girl there was nothing wrong with him other than being a dirty old man.'

'As long as you say so,' Robert rejoined.

'I do and unless we want to lose our advantage let's get moving again. This time we want to advertise our presence much less, so you get into the back Robert and keep as low a profile as possible.

She turned to Hella who nodded: 'Front passenger seat and keep out of sight. I know.'

So off they went, turning right onto the main road and right again at the first traffic lights much to Robert's confusion.

'I thought we were going to East Midlands Airport,' he observed.

'We are,' Rita replied taking the first left and then left again.

As they approached the traffic lights on the main street, a police car raced across, siren blaring. Robert immediately started to panic.

'How did they find out?' he cried. 'You said it could be hours before the others made contact.'

'For goodness sake pull yourself together,' Rita turned and snapped at him. 'They could be after anyone,' Hella pointed out. 'It doesn't have to be us.'

'But what if they see the Bentley parked at the garage?'

Rita shook her head in disbelief. 'How could they when it's already being stripped down for the overhaul?'

Although Robert didn't say anything more for fear of further reaction, he decided to keep his own counsel unless something else happened to prove him right.

So the unlikely trio swept over the crossroads as the lights changed and Rita drove them out into the open countryside in the general direction of the airport. Several miles further on Robert had no choice but to break the silence again.

'I thought we were going to East Midlands Airport,' he said.

'We are,' Rita replied. 'What makes you think we aren't?'

'We just passed a sign to it, pointing in the opposite direction.'

Rita slammed on the brakes and gave him a broadside.

'Right Mr. Know-all. You know so much. You take us there. Come on.'

She started to open her door, but Robert, ever the wimp and almost glad to be under the thumb, put his hand on her shoulder.

'No! No! I just saw the sign and thought …'

'Well don't think! OK! Do you think I would drive straight up to the main entrance and announce our presence to security? I know all this is alien to you and you've led a sheltered life, but really!'

Poor old Robert. He didn't know where to put himself as usual. 'Sorry. I'm just not used to all this.'

His tone was so pathetic that Rita relented. She wondered what kind of an ogre Grace was to have subjugated him like this. 'Forget it,' she said. 'Just leave me to do the thinking.'

He didn't reply, but Hella added: 'Be like me. Go with the flow.'

Nothing more was said until they reached the far perimeter of the airport. Rita turned into a gateway from which a well-used track stretched away across a couple of fields towards the main body of buildings. She got out, opened the gate, drove through and then shut and locked it behind them before heading off towards their destination.

'So far so good,' she sighed as they approached another gate. This was the final hurdle to be cleared by the intrepid trio before reaching Rita and Jack's main Stearman stunt bi-plane.

But prior to that Robert was unable to stop himself from pointing to the dark figure waiting for them by the gate.

'Who's that?' he asked the doubtful tone quite clear in his voice.

But despite his misgivings Rita only chuckled rather cheekily. 'Don't worry about him,' she replied. 'That's Joe Brennan. He's on our side.'

'What about all those police and security men milling around outside departures and presumably more on the inside?' her devil's advocate pointed out.

'Ah Robert. It seems that underneath that clown's costume you're more observant than I thought.'

'So what are we going to do now?'

Even Hella was beginning to show signs of panic.

'We wait and see what Joe has to say. Then we get the shit our of here!'

This brought an unusual wry remark from Robert, who at last seemed to have resigned himself to the situation.

'No problem then. We just do as we have been doing and leave even more people in chaos!'

Somewhat relieved that Robert was beginning to see the funny side of their predicament, neither Rita nor Hella said anything.

Instead Rita concentrated on driving through the gate as Joe opened it and then waited for him to jump into the back seat alongside Robert.

'I like the clown but the show girl's even better,' he chortled, settling down as Rita put her foot down again.

'Never mind that,' she cried. 'What's the current plan?'

Joe shook his head anxiously. 'I tried to fob them off for as long as I could but they're sending a couple of cars over anyway.'

'So how long have we got? Realistically?' she demanded.

'Well, they'll have to use the perimeter track, so I would say about ten minutes at best.'

'I agree.'

Within seconds they were parked behind the Stearman ready to get out of the car and board the plane.

'Sorry about the wing-walk,' Rita told Robert. 'No time to set it up. You can have a free one later.'

'I don't think so, but thanks for the offer,' said the mightily relieved clown.

'Oh well, suit yourself. Now get your butts on to that aircraft while I sort things out with Joe.'

She turned to the airport private area manager who had a half incredulous smile on his face.

'Will you be OK?'

'Yeh! I'll be fine. You overpowered me and made me do what you wanted, didn't you? Just tell me what you want me to say and get going. The plane is all prepared and ready for take-off, although I don't know how you're going to achieve that. They've grounded everything until further notice.'

'I'll manage somehow,' said Rita a little tentatively.

'Knowing you I know you will.' They were interrupted by the sound of a police siren drawing ominously near and Rita immediately raced to the Stearman.

'Thanks for everything,' she called out to him. I'll pay you later.'

She was interrupted by another ear-splitting noise; the arrival of a Boeing 737-800 from Malaga.

Joe's reply was drowned by the roar of the powerful jet engines using reverse thrust to slow it down.

'I know you will,' he said to himself. 'And I look forward to it.'

Rita knew what he had said instinctively and as she started up the Stearman and taxied towards the open gate she gave him a wave and a look which told him everything he needed to know.

CHAPTER 7

As the bright yellow bi-plane began to pick up speed away from the private compound and Joe was closing the gate behind them as nonchalantly as possible, a veritable horde of airport police, local police, security staff and others burst through the other entrance.

Pausing only to get their bearings they knocked him flying, flung open the gate again and set off in pursuit.

One officer helped Joe to his feet and yelled: 'Is that them?'

'Who?' Joe cried, dusting himself off and still pretending to be flabbergasted. 'What the hell is going on?'

The man was becoming even more agitated as his colleagues and company raced away from them.

'The clown and the two birds!'

'Birds?'

'Girls! You know! Are you taking the micky?'

'Now would I do that?' muttered Joe rather too condescendingly. But then realised that he mustn't push it too far or even this bloke would catch on.

'Oh sorry. You mean the barnstormers of course.'

The officer shook his head and stamped his foot. 'Who the heck did you think I meant, the ruddy Queen or somebody?'

Joe resisted the temptation to admonish him for not showing more respect for our sovereign and replied: 'Yes. The barnstormers. That's them.' He pointed to the departing stunt plane.

This infuriated the man even more. 'I know it is.'

'Well why did you ask me then if you knew all the time?'

'Right. That's it!' cried the officer as Joe's tactics finally dawned on him. His next question was slowed right down as if he were talking to an imbecile. 'I – simply – want – to – know – where – they – are – going. Can – you – understand – that?'

'Ah. Yes. No.' Joe saw the man's expression darken even more and decided enough was enough. 'No. I mean yes. Birmingham. Yes I'm sure that is their destination.'

'Didn't they have any papers …?' the officer started then thought better of it. 'Never-mind now. I'll be back to see you later.'

'I can't wait,' Joe murmured under his breath as the frustrated man tugged the mobile phone out of his pocket and punched in his leader's number.

The rest of the posse were now too far away to shout to but apparently no nearer the speeding aircraft. When his phone rang the leader of the pack had hesitated and the second officer ran into him. Several more were running too quickly to stop and soon there was a whole pile of them scrambling around on the hard concrete roadway.

Way ahead in the Stearman Hella was looking back anxiously and then began chuckling. 'Don't worry about the police,' she laughed. 'It's like the Keystone Cops back there.'

But Rita wasn't interested in the Keystone Cops at that moment. She was more concerned about the heroic but foolhardy baggage cart driver who had parked his vehicle directly in front of them trying to prevent them from taking off. Any lesser pilot would have had no option but to crash into it. But she was no lesser pilot. She was also well-versed in stunt flying. Without even an unnecessary thought she gunned the throttle at the same time as pulling back the joystick. Any other bi-plane couldn't have done it, but this one did. Well almost. The wheels just clipped the top of the piled up cases, causing the whole lot to topple off the cart onto the ground. Most of them withstood the impact, but some spilled underwear in all directions. Surprisingly not all the frills and laces came out of the women's baggage either.

The Stearman bounced down onto the concrete again, but Rita didn't even have a second to relax before Robert was screeching like a maniac.

'For heaven's sake lookout!'

It didn't take her even another second to see the huge Boeing 737-800 baring down on them as it taxied towards the Arrivals park.

'Assume the crash position. Here we go again!'

CHAPTER 7

Her companions didn't need any second bidding. They bent forwards, heads between their legs, arms braced and awaited what seemed to be the inevitable smash. But as always Rita had an answer. With a wing and a prayer she bounced the aircraft back into the sky, swerving to their right as she did so. Fortunately the airline pilot veered to his right and although he ended up stuck in the mud with a badly damaged undercarriage a fatal accident was averted.

Meanwhile the Stearman completed a smooth arc over the airport buildings before flipping over to the left as though setting a course for Birmingham. Rita climbed to around five thousand feet so that they would be easy to follow by radar. The radio began to crackle and she yanked a handful of wires out of their sockets.

'Oh dear!' she cried. 'Now we won't be able to let anyone know where we are going.'

Although Hella appreciated the humorous irony of their situation, Robert didn't. He was more concerned about what might happen than throwing their pursuers off the scent.

'What happens if we do crash?' he demanded, already glad he had buckled himself into his seat belt even if he had unfolded from the crash position.

Rita couldn't help but let out a little chuckle. 'Actually that is what we are going to do.'

'But we haven't got any parachutes,' Hella cut in.

'At the level we'll be flying they wouldn't be any use anyway.'

Suddenly Robert came to life again. Rita knew he wouldn't be able to maintain his silence for long.

'If you think I'm going to jump out of a plane in mid-air, with or without a parachute you're very much mistaken,' he said, his voice sounding as though he was keeping calm only with the greatest effort.

Beneath her own apparent relaxed expression Rita had felt the excitement inside her building up to an explosive climax. It was better than sex could ever be even though it did involve shaking the male of the species to the core. That climax was on the brink of the greatest thrill she had ever known.

'Well?' Robert wanted to know.

'Well,' laughed Rita, enjoying herself to the full. 'If you think you've had some hair-raising experiences prepare for the worst!'

Then, before either of them could say another word she dipped the nose down, swooped below five hundred feet and then sparred back up into an almost vertical climb. This was just the start of the manoeuvre but Hella's stomach seemed to have risen into her throat and plummeted back down to her feet. Robert? Well Robert was Robert. He just sat there with a glazed expression on his face wondering what really was going to happen.

He soon found out!

At the top of the climb, over five thousand feet, Rita stalled the Stearman, dipped to the left and sent the aircraft into a falling spin, apparently out of control. The ground rushed up to meet them as the sky and horizon flashed round in circles and Robert waited for the end, paralysed with terror. But in fact the highly skilled stunt pilot knew exactly what she was doing. A fraction of a second before it was too late, she pulled out of the aerobatic manoeuvre and raced along into another wide turn just above tree top level.

If the East Midlands Airport's radar had been able to locate and track them, which it couldn't now, it would have revealed that they were now heading north west.

Still keeping her visual focus on their low level tree skimming Rita half turned and called out to her two passengers: 'Was that enough excitement for you then?'

'There was no reply.

'Robert! Hello!'

Nothing.

She checked that no unforeseen obstacles were looming up in front of them. Then she glanced over he right shoulder to see Hella hanging over the edge of her open seat, hands dangling, head lolling. She had obviously fainted at some point during the spin and was still out.

After checking the front again Rita repeated the process with regard to Robert. She had to smile, but not unkindly. The poor fellow was frozen solid with shock in his seat, eyes like wide sightless orbs, mouth gaping, tongue tied.

Despite her concern for them Rita had no choice but to complete her low level flight plan.

∼

Back at the airport radar operators were confused. Twice in a short time their target vanished off the screen. The blip reappeared quickly after the first disappearance, but then vanished again during a series of erratic aerobatics.

One baffled observer commented: 'We can't be absolutely sure but it looks as if they could have crashed.'

The longer the Stearman was off screen the more likely they were to have come to grief. Eventually it was decided to launch a search and rescue helicopter.

'We can only hope they will either locate the fugitives or find the wreckage,' Grace and the rest of the makeshift posse were told. 'It won't be easy as we aren't entirely sure of their route.'

Grace's reply was said to be unreportable by the assembled journalists as were similar comments by Jack and Hella's maniac of a partner.

∼

Unaware of all this, Rita flew on as quickly as possible. Soon they reached the edge of forests planted to regenerate mining scars on the increasingly mountainous landscape. Among the trees was a network of roads once used by opencast mining machinery. These were just wide enough with woodlands densely packed on either side for her to hurtle along almost at ground level. Once or twice as the aircraft twisted and turned, buffeted by strong gusts of wind, she thought the wheels would touch the ground, either being torn off or sending them spinning to be smashed to pieces in the trees. Before she could collect her thoughts again there was a wild animal-like howl from behind her. Uncharacteristically she had allowed her mind to wander.

'For heaven's sake, look out!'

Imminent mortal danger had caused a rapid thaw in his brain and it was what saved their lives. Snapped back into full focus Rita just had time to swerve the Stearman round a tight right-hand corner as the dense wall of trees seemed to be rushing towards them. There was no time for relief however, as the road almost immediately swung back to the left. Once the cartoon-like visions of Hella and Robert being flung from side to side like harnessed rag dolls had faded from her brain, she was finally able to calm down and look ahead along the tree-lined approach to the small runway that was their destination on this leg of their journey.

A glance back revealed poor Robert trying desperately to haul the now panicking Hella back into a more comfortable position. Rita saw the funny side of it, but also appreciated his efforts. Sure that he would succeed her attention returned to their destination. At the far end of the airstrip stood a large impressive mansion with extensive outbuildings. She even allowed herself some measure of satisfaction knowing it would take a while for their pursuers to find out whether or not they had crashed and if not, which direction she had taken and where they were now.

However her reverie was cut short not by any form of pursuit, but a plaintiff plea from Robert.

'Pardon me for asking but I wonder whether it might be possible for us to be set down for a while, just to sit and reflect where we've been and where we go from here?'

He finished with a deep sigh and Hella her voice still taut with tension added: 'I'll drink to that.'

'You won't have to wait long now,' Rita reassured them,. 'We'll be landing soon.'

'Thank goodness for that,' said Hella before Robert cut in again.

'There is just one more small matter however. Well, it's not all that small actually.'

'What's that?' Rita asked in all innocence.

'There's a bloody great house looming up in front of us. How are you going to get over that?'

'I'm not,' she chuckled.

'You certainly won't get round it,' cried Hella.

'I know that,' laughed Rita.

'You've heard of short take-off and landing aircraft haven't you?'

'I suppose so.'

'Well I propose to put this crate down on the front lawn or near enough to it.'

Without another word she eased the wheels gently and taxied over the lush green grass, turning and coming to a surprisingly gentle halt near the bottom of the stone steps leading up to the grand front entrance.

'There you are. Safely back on terra firma,' Rita chuckled. 'Didn't I do well?'

But Robert was back to his role as devil's advocate. 'Great. And what is the owner of this place going to say now that we've cut up his expensive lawn and parked outside his front door?'

'Not a lot,' Rita replied confidently. 'I would imagine he'll be too pleased to see me.' She paused for effect and then added: 'Anyway you'll soon find out. Here he comes now.'

As she spoke one of the ornate double doors swung open and out came a jovial looking gentleman in his fifties with a huge smile on his aristocratic features and his arms stretched out to welcome them.

'Rita my dear. How nice to see you again my dear. Though I must admit I was becoming rather worried about you. You're causing quite a stir on the news. They think you've had a prang.'

'What me?' she laughed. 'Surely you know me better than that!'

This seemed to amuse him no end and he chortled along with her for a while before saying: 'More about that later my dear. Go and park your lovely Stearman in its usual place in the museum, then bring your two charming friends through to the house for tea. That will give us the opportunity to plan the next stage of your incredible journey.'

So saying he turned on his heels and returned through the door with a friendly wave behind him. Rita restarted the engine and set out to do as he had said.

'Wow!' gasped an obviously impressed Hella. 'You do seem to move in an amazing variety of circles. Who was that?'

'That my girl was none other than Lord Harry Honington, owner of the Honington Aircraft Museum, probably second only to Beaulieu; aviator and world famous hot-air balloonist.'

'Oh no!' sobbed Robert in absolute horror. 'No! Definitely not! No way am I going up in a balloon! Not even for you!'

'We shall see,' Rita murmured just low enough so that he couldn't hear her. 'We shall see.'

CHAPTER 8

There was a convenient space for the Stearman to be parked near the entrance to the museum's main exhibition hall with a little help from a mechanic working on a nearby Sopwith Camel biplane. Once in place no-one would even suspect that Rita's aircraft wasn't a permanent part of the collection. It seemed that the stunt plane was as authentic as all the other historic exhibits which it was until the barnstormer restored it into the flying phenomenon used in their displays.

Robert, who had been a keen plane spotter in his youth, was really in his element. There was a time when his grand father worked as a batman at RAF College Cranwell in Lincolnshire and he had access to 'top secret' aircraft recognition manuals, that he claimed to be able to identify any plane in the world just by its silhouette in the sky.

Now he was in the heaven of his boyhood dreams. In the far right-hand corner of the converted hangar was a Fairey Swordfish complete with torpedo, beside a stubby little Gloster Gladiator and one of the most beautiful of all bi-planes, a de-Havilland Tiger Moth. He was just contemplating the amphibian lines of a Catalina flying boat when his reverie was interrupted by the appearance of their host in the doorway. Lord Honington beckoned them to follow him across the pebbled courtyard and into the main house.

'We'll take tea in the duke's room,' he told them. 'Then we can discuss your best course of action.'

They were ushered into what amounted to a lavishly furnished sitting room with classic paintings hung on each papered wall. A rather effeminate young man showed them to their seats and offered them tea and fancy cakes. The china service looked so delicate and exquisite it must have cost hundreds if not thousands of pounds. Hella gave Robert a reassuring smile as she raised the cup to her full lips while he hesitated, terrified he might drop his drink, at worst breaking the priceless vessel or at best spilling tea on the thick piled Persian carpet. Fortunately neither of these materialised and they settled into their crucial discussion.

Lord Honington's first act was to introduce them to the young man who had welcomed them.

'This is my partner Julian. He makes the finest cakes in Christendom, don't you my dear?'

'Too true,' said Rita.

'Not half,' Hella added.

'Charmed, I'm sure,' quipped the obviously flattered Henry.

Robert said nothing, but kept his own counsel about Henry. He wasn't used to coming into contact with such characters and decided a polite silence was the best policy. Henry gave his a somewhat quizzical smile and departed to refill the solid silver teapot. People like Honington's partner did not usually feature in Robert's previously closeted existence and the few who did tended to be avoided, though in a polite rather than unreasonable fashion.

Meanwhile the irrepressible Lord had been speaking while Robert had been lost in his daydreams.

'So what do you think?'

The question caught Robert totally unawares and he floundered: 'I – er – yes; that seems like a good idea to me.'

'I thought you said nobody would ever get you in a balloon?' Rita cut in.

The noble Lord, ever the diplomat, added: 'Well it won't be possible to fly until the thermals are right early tomorrow morning so you will be able to sleep on it.'

'Not that it will make any difference,' Hella laughed. 'We're all in this together and you'll do what we say in the end.'

There was a brief but embarrassing silence as Robert decided now was not the time to launch into one of his famous failed arguments. Eventually Honington was the first to speak again.

'So Blackpool it is, though I cannot for the life of me think why!'

'Blackpool!'

Robert almost choked on his fairy cake.

'Safety in anonymity,' muttered Rita.

'You'll love it where we're headed,' Hella chuckled.

'I would, most definitely!' A highly suggestive remark from Henry who had returned from the kitchen.

'More tea anyone?' Followed by a strong brandy to help you sleep?'

'Sleep!' echoed Robert. It's only early evening yet.'

But Honington, ever the pragmatist, would hear none of it.

'After what you three have been through you will need all the rest you can get. And not only have we got to be up before dawn tomorrow, but there will also be a hard flight ahead of us.'

This brought no further response from Robert who saw no logical reason to argue for the moment. He accepted the cognac gratefully and sat back to drink it.

'There's a good boy,' coaxed Henry. 'Make sure you get your beauty sleep.'

The others laughed suggestively, but Robert felt he didn't exactly get the point of the insinuation. Best not to show it he thought. While they finished their drinks Lord Harry explained a few of the finer points of ballooning with particular emphasis on the do's and don'ts of the sport.

'You'll love it once we're in free flight. The experience of a lifetime,' he said. The girls chorused their approval, but Robert was less enthusiastic in his reply.

'I can't wait,' he mumbled.

Eventually the visitors said goodnight to Lord Honington and were taken to their respective bedrooms by the ever helpful Henry.

'This is your chamber,' he told Robert. 'The Prince's bedroom. You really will feel like royalty. You will find more suitable clothing for a balloon flight than that rather charming but ridiculous clown's costume you are wearing.'

Robert dreaded to think what Henry meant by 'more suitable' but was so taken aback by the splendour of the room, he could hardly speak. It was the most exotic, no, erotic place Robert had ever seen, even though the latter was not a word he was used to using in his genteel world. Every item of furniture seemed to have been made with a different aspect of love-making in mind – chases longues, welcoming easy chairs, man-sized ottoman, sprawling bean bags and a plush carpet with at least a six-inch pile, soft enough for any kind of a romp involving any number of bodies. The walls were hung with life-size portraits of nubile young women in the most compromising poses. The overall crimson and black décor including the bed – and what a bed! The most Robert had ever seen! A giant king size plus four-poster with soft silken sheets and matching semi-transparent drapes – just waiting for him to strip off, leap into and satisfy the lust for sleep which was beginning to engulf his whole being after his long ordeal and the effects of one of the most potent brandies he had ever tasted.

'A sudden spate of giggles from the doorway interrupted his reverie.

'Just your kind of room,' Hella chuckled.

'And How!' laughed Rita.

'would you like a hand with your costume?' Henry chimed in. 'It's so cute and Lord Honington says I'm the best valet he's ever had.'

Much to the amusement of the two girls, Robert's features flooded with a mixture of shock horror and embarrassment.

'Oh – er – no! No thanks. I can manage,' he choked.

Henry who was also going along with the situation half in hope and half in fun, smiled. 'Ah well. Suit yourself. But you only have to pull the bell cord if you do need me at any time.'

All three of them howled as the would-be valet closed the door and left Robert in some kind of peace, if only temporarily. All he wanted to do at that moment was to move the next day's change of clothes onto a chair, take off and discard the clown's costume which had caused him so much embarrassment and get into that sumptuously inviting bed. This he did in double quick time and as soon as his head touched the satin covered pillow he was dead to the world.

Had he stayed awake long enough to see the girls established in their rooms the former clown would have been impressed by the harem style décor.

'Full of eastern promise,' commented Hella.

'Worthy of a sultana's boudoir,' added Rita. 'Oh Robert. If you could only see us now!'

CHAPTER 8

So they too turned in and Henry returned to his household duties whatever they might be.

'Poor old Robert,' smiled Hella. 'I believe the noble Lord told him the room not only belonged to a former Prince of Wales, but that it was also haunted by the wayward royal's ghost.'

'That remains to be seen,' Rita replied with a knowing smile before going to her own bedroom. 'We shall have to see what materializes.'

Meanwhile Robert was sound asleep. He continued to be so until the darkest hours just after midnight. Then his slumber was disturbed by what sounded like a furtive movement At first he thought it was part of the spectacular dream he had been having about an Indiana Jones type escape from death in a hot air balloon. But the next noise, almost below the level of hearing, brought his wide awake. It was as if someone or something was shuffling through the thick pile of the carpet towards him!

Visions of the erstwhile Prince of Wales with his 'head tucked underneath his arm' bending over the bed looking to see who had dared to usurp his lustful throne flashed through his mind.

Execution in the bloody tower! Robert waited with proverbial baited breath, straining to catch any slight sight or sound of the intruder from his frozen position between the deceptively soft silken sheets.

If the others learned of his illogical fears they would ridicule him even more than usual.

More tiny noises sent his nerves soaring to level red. Was that a pitiful sob? A choking spasm of rage? Or what? If only the room wasn't so dark. Black, impenetrable nothingness; an abyss of silence. How could he fight what he couldn't see or hear?

Whispers? Murmurs of a homicidal phantom?

Suddenly the bed moved slightly as if it had been nudged involuntarily, sending Robert's taut nerves into an even worse state of paralysis.

Another terror hit him.

What if it wasn't a ghost at all? What if Lord Harry Honington was in fact some kind of latter day Sweeney Todd, trapping his victims and then slaughtering them like pigs to put in a pie?

Now he was really letting his imagination run away with him. Even Robert himself managed a smile at such an outrageous suggestion.

His smile was cut short by another movement.

Merciful heavens! What if the bed was a murderous trap. Another infinitesimal sound made him imagine it collapsing into the floor plunging him and the sheets and blankets into a dank cellar below where Henry was waiting with a big cleaver to cut him up into little pieces before feeding him to the cooking pot.

Ridiculous?

But there were precedents and American film star Johnny Depp had even made a musical out of them.

Henry?

Well the genial Lord Harry would hardly do his own dirty work when he had such a nice man to do it for him.

Nice man? Henry? Oh no! That would be even more frightening. The loveable valet had obviously set his sights on him. Could he be the unwelcome visitor creeping around the Prince's boudoir like a wraith in the middle of the night?

Without warning the tension increased to an even more unbearable pitch as Robert Sensed movement to his right.

Someone was fumbling with the bedclothes, lifting them up ever so gently and slipping in beside him! This was too much! He couldn't bear it any longer. He was just about to draw back his leg and kick the interloper onto the floor when a brief chuckle stopped him.

Sensual hands moved temptingly over his naked body.

Gentle hands but definitely female hands.

Hella!

Her chuckles were louder and more prolonged now. Robert was torn between embarrassment and outrage, with a certain amount of temptation thrown in, which shocked him even more.

As his enjoyment increased against his better judgement Robert was in for another even bigger shock. The darkness was still absolute but now there was a disturbance to his left. The covers there were lifted high enough to admit another body alongside him. Two more sets of fingers fluttered across and up and down his body accompanied by a somewhat deeper more meaningful bout of laughing.

Seconds later it was pandemonium. The girls were all over Robert. He was wriggling violently half enjoying it and half trying to break free and preserve his modesty. It was too late for that now of course but he was too panic stricken to realise how much he had changed since encountering his two tormentors. Not so much changed but having his inner self propelled to the surface. In other words his whole image of respectability in tatters. Shrieking with laughter Rita rolled on top of him. Robert rolled over back onto her but his momentum sent them both tumbling to the floor. Both of them had the wind knocked out of them and as they lay flat on their backs gasping Hella's face appeared over the edge of the bed, a look of triumph shining all over her lovely features.

'You know what they call that carpet?' she cried. 'Shag pile!'

Then with a flourish and a wild howl of 'Geronimo!' she threw herself down on top of them.

Rita managed to roll out of the way at the last second but Robert had the stuffing knocked out of him once again.

Before there could be any further damage someone knocked loudly on the bedroom door.

Still unable to control her mirth Rita hauled herself to her feet and staggered across to open it. She turned the key, the door swung wide to reveal the ever faithful Henry his own expression a mixture of amusement, humour and helpfulness.

'Sorry to interrupt your fun and games,' he said. 'In other circumstances I might be tempted to join in. But Lord Honington has asked me to inform you that a police car has just arrived and he would be grateful if you could tone down the noise in case they discover you are here. The last thing he would want them to think is that he was aiding and abetting a gang of dangerous criminals.

CHAPTER 9

Henry had only been gone for a couple of minutes before he was back again looking unusually ruffled for him as if he had run all the way upstairs, which he had. For a while he was choking and spluttering so much no words would come, but a heavy smack on the back by Rita brought him out of it. The blow sent Henry staggering into Robert who recoiled as if he had been electrocuted. But the unwilling valet kept his balance somehow stuttering: 'R-really! T-there's no n-need for that.'

'So what do we need?' Rita demanded as Robert continued to be dumbstruck and Hella gnawed at her wrist to keep from bursting with laughter.

Recovering his composure Henry glared at them and snorted: 'You won't find it so funny when I tell you what has happened.'

'Go on then. We're all ears,' said Rita.

'Speak for yourself,' added Robert, finally coming back to life.

'Speak for myself I might do,' Henry retorted. 'But this is about you three, not me. And there is no time to lose.'

'For heaven's sake get on with it!' Rita cried.

'All right! All right! Keep your shirt on! Oh sorry. None of you are wearing anything at the moment are you?'

An angry glare from Rita spurred him on.

'Sorry. The police want to search the house. Apparently one of them saw a light on in an upstairs window and they are concerned about our safety.'

'I assure you we are not violent criminals,' Robert was horrified.

'Not to our friends anyway,' laughed Hella.

'According to the law you have left a trail of destruction stretching back to Nottingham that would be worthy of American gangsters.'

This was the moment for Rita to interrupt.

'Things are not always what they seem. What we need is a place to hide.'

'Which is exactly why I'm here,' Henry explained and without another word he strode over to a life-size painting of a beautiful naked woman. Before any of them could question his actions, he reached up to the woman's prominent right nipple. This he tweaked firmly.

'Oh! Come on …' Rita began, but was stopped by an ominous click in the wall behind the picture. It caught everyone's attention and their eyes widened collectively as the painting swung outwards to reveal a small dark room which was little more than a recess.

A priest's hole incorporated into the original house when it was built.

'Voilà!' gestured Henry with a dramatic flourish.

'No! Definitely not! If you think you're getting me into that cramped space with these two sex maniacs you're very much mistaken,' Robert insisted.

But his words were curtailed by the sound of approaching voices somewhere on the staircase. This sent Henry into a veritable tantrum.

'For goodness sake do as you're told immediately!' he cried.

With that he gave Robert an almighty shove which sent him sprawling into what was virtually a large cupboard as far as space was concerned. An instant later the girls had tumbled in on top of him.

Robert howled with a mixture of pain and indignity as Henry closed the secret door behind them.

'And keep the noise down whatever you do,' hissed Henry. If they hear anything it will only be a matter of time before they find you!'

Then he turned away to sort out the bed clothes before the police arrived.

In the priest's hole it was utter chaos if only in hushed tones.

'Listen,' Rita urged Robert as he continued to thrash about like a fish on dry land. 'I'll make a deal with you. We won't bother you if you don't bother us.'

Although he didn't actually answer it seemed obvious that he had no choice but to agree. There was a short spell of shuffling, a pause of silence and then more scuffling followed by a sudden howl from Hella.

'I thought we had a mutual agreement,' she sobbed.

'Sorry,' Robert replied somewhat embarrassed. 'It was an accident.'

'Accident or not, that is not the place to poke a young lady.'

'Sorry,' Robert repeated. 'Where is that?'

'In the eye,' moaned Hella.

Finally Rita had had enough of their banter.

'Shut up will you? I think they are just about to enter your bedroom. Do you want to be discovered?'

No-one answered, which was as well because the police and Lord Harry did in fact enter the room at the moment.

'What was that?' asked one of the constables.

'Yes,' added his colleague. 'I thought I heard something too.'

The quick thinking Lord Honington had an immediate explanation ready.

'Rats. In the walls. We're plagued with them at the moment.

Without further comment the policemen made a quick but thorough investigation of the room going even as far as to climb up and look on top of the four poster as well as under the bed.

'Pot needs emptying,' said the senior officer, then saw Lord Harry's horrified expression which he fortunately saw as a personal reproach rather than guilt. 'Sorry mi lord. Only joking.'

Although the two policemen listened hard before leaving the bedroom there were no more suspicious sounds from within the walls, maybe because the three fugitives were holding their breath until their lungs were almost at breaking point. Cramp was also setting in due to their enforced immobility. How Robert managed to stop his leg going into a violent spasm and dealing Rita an injury he'll never know.

It was some time before the secret door swung open to free the trio of prisoners from their hidey hole. Robert shot out as if fired from a catapult. As the two girls struggled to regain their composure he rolled about on the floor clutching at his calf muscles and trying to massage them back to normal while simultaneously striving to unlock his back from the crick that had developed in the confined wall space.

In an effort to help him Henry, who had opened the door, tried to straighten Robert's right leg and stretch the foot to ease the cramp only to be met with cries of pain and frustration.

CHAPTER 9

When the furore quietened down enough for him to be heard Henry told them: 'As any chance of sleep has now been lost Lord Honington requests you to get dressed and join him downstairs for an early breakfast.'

'What about the police?' Rita wanted to know.

'Gone for now, but they were very suspicious of your aircraft being parked in the collection and it wouldn't surprise me if they are not too far away, ready to return at the slightest sign of dubious activity.'

'So what do we do?' asked Robert.

'What his lordship tells you,' was the immediate reply.

It didn't take the three fugitives long to comply with Lord Harry's breakfast invitation and they were soon downstairs tucking into an appetising full English meal of bacon, egg, sausage, beans, tomatoes and – much to Robert's disgust – black pudding. Henry attended to coffee refills while they received their instructions on how to make a success of a balloon flight. Hot air the prime motivation.

Throughout the discussions Robert still insisted that nothing on earth would persuade him to climb into such an exposed basket.

'Would you rather remain here and face the police?' asked Rita.

'Maybe it won't come to that. They could have gone elsewhere,' he was totally unconvincing in his reply and they all knew it, even he himself.'

After breakfast and final preparations for inflating the hot air balloon into its easily recognisable pink elephant shape work continued to get it into tethered take-off readiness.

'Once we're sure of the right thermals we can get under way,' Lord Harry told them.

With a helping hand from Henry the two girls climbed up the short rope ladder and into the basket alongside the arch-balloonist Lord Harry.

His valet beckoned Robert to follow suit, but the last potential passenger still hesitated.

'Last call,' shouted Lord Honington and after a short pause cast off with a disappointed flourish. The balloon inched away and upwards but as it did so Robert suddenly changed his mind on seeing and hearing a police car racing up the drive towards him.

'Too late!' cried the pilot. But Robert was determined and helped by Henry he managed to reach the bottom rungs of the rope, twisting his arms into a firm but agonising hold and hanging on for dear life.

The police arrived just too late to grab his dangling feet and were left fuming on the ground below. Danger, however, seemed to have hijacked his incredible life, so it was not surprising to see a tall fir tree looming up in front of him. Helped by a frantic burst of flame from the burner the balloon soared just high enough for his feet to crash through the foliage like a Grand National horse blasting through Bencher's Brook at Braintree. Then as an even higher line of trees appeared ahead Lord Harry called down to him: 'Climb up you bloody fool! Come on!'

An instant later he was about to tell Robert not to look down, he realised he already had!

Robert looked up again grimly clinging on desperately.

'I can't!' he yelled. 'I daren't move!'

Lord Harry shouted down to him as one arm began to slip: 'Hang on! We'll haul you up! Don't look down,' he cried again , but once again Robert already had and began wriggling and squirming in sheer panic.

'Come on you two. Give me a hand,' his lordship told the girls. 'We've got to get him up here before he lets go!'

What with Robert's dangling weight and the currents of air as the balloon continued on its way it seemed impossible but somehow they hoisted him high enough for Lord Honington to reach over and pull him over the side and into the basket where he lay gasping and shaking with fear and exhaustion. Hella knelt down beside him, mopping his forehead and trying to calm him down. She understood that Robert wasn't by any means a coward, but someone whose whole well-ordered life had been utterly upskittled by events that had sent reality out of the window.

Once he had regained his composure as far as could be in the circumstances, there were several questions on his kind. Not least about the balloon itself.

'Why is it shaped like a sausage?' he wanted to know. 'Is it more aerodynamic or something?' At this Rita bent down and put her hand on his shoulder.

'It;s not a sausage darling. Take another look,; she urged.

The noble lord had a puzzled almost undefinable expression on his face while Hella burst into floods of laughter.

Realisation suddenly dawned on the hapless Robert who blushed to livid red. But Rita let out a playful chuckle.

'Don't worry. It isn't what you think. Lord Harry is into farm foods in a big way and the balloon is simple a novel way of advertising his pork sausages.'

This seemed to settle Lord Honington's reservations about what she was going yo say. He even permitted himself a satisfied smile and a quick burst on the burner to increase their height.

'So,' said a much more relaxed Robert. 'I suppose we can settle down for a gentle ride in your beautiful balloon. Or is that too much to ask?'

Although he smiled in the most genial kind of way, the irony of their situation was not lost on the noble lord, who nodded in guarded agreement, but replied: 'That's if we can shake off the procession of police cars, army vehicles, vans, pick-up trucks and automobiles currently trying to keep pace with us along the roads.'

To which the ever alert Rita added ominously: And of course the Apache strike helicopter closing in rapidly from starboard!'

CHAPTER 10

'Plus that lot up ahead,' Robert choked, pointing to a dozen or more hot air balloons all shaped like sausages and all bearing down on them like a stately fleet of old fashioned galleons.

'Now we're really sunk!' Rita quipped.

But Lord Honington shook his head. His beaming smile caught them all by surprise, but was undeniably infectious.

'Not at all my dear friends. Not at all. This is what I've been waiting for; our escape escort.'

'How can a group of sausage shaped balloons hope to fight off a fully armed helicopter!' Robert was as sceptical as ever.

'Not fight them off dear boy. Haven't you heard of the shoal syndrome?'

'What have fish got to do with it?' Hella asked, as confused as Robert was.

Rita, however, had sussed it out before either of them.

'I know what you mean,' she said. 'Shoals of fish stick together to outwit predators like sharks.'

The noble lord rubbed his hands together with glee.

'That's right, although in this case they will only be here to confuse the issue.'

'Isn't it confused enough?' Robert grumbled.

'The more confused the better, I say.'

Hella, as usual, was enjoying every minute. She clearly thrived on excitement, even danger as long as it was not too threatening.

'So your friends are going to make us difficult to detect,' commented Rita. 'You do always seem to have an answer to everything.'

Before she could say anything else the crowd of sausage balloons were milling round them like a swarm of sex-starved midges over a river. The Apache helicopter simply hovered ominously while they sorted themselves out, then followed at a safe distance as they drifted off to the north west. Even with its presence and the continued pursuit of vehicles on the ground the atmosphere was more relaxed. Lord Harry had such a confident aura in all that he did which made it difficult for his passengers not to share his enthusiasm. But some doubts began to grow when they floated into a mountainous area and one balloon dropped away towards the ground below. Seconds later it was gone through one of the many valley features among the hills.

Lord Honington turned to look at the helicopter which didn't even waver off its course at all. On they flew around a huge rock face. For a few seconds they were out of sight of the Apache while the ground posse had no choice other than to follow the winding road through the mountains. The interval gave another sausage the chance to drift away from the fleeing group. But the result was the same. The dogged helicopter pilot refused to be diverted from its course.

This brought a more serious expression to the noble lord's face. He was clearly troubled by the helicopter pilot's apparent ability to ascertain quite definitely whether or not his balloon was still in the pack.

'There is something wrong here,' he told them. 'They seem to have a perfect way of making sure we are still in the main formation.'

'Maybe they have the ability to pinpoint this balloon as opposed to all the others,' Robert ventured.]

'That could be true my boy. But there is no difference between them. These balloons were all designed and donated to the International Federation as a specific racing class. I assure you they are all identical … Unless …

'Unless what?' Rita wanted to know.

'Unless … Just a moment. Do any of you have cell phones with you?'

'Not me,' said Rita.

'Not guilty milord,' Hella added.

But Robert said nothing.

'It's you, isn't it?' Hella berated him.

'But I thought you threw it away,' Rita pointed out.

'I did, but I do have another one with me. It's quite special.'

'Not special enough to be immune from tracking,' the noble lord cut in.

Robert hadn't a clue of course. He simply used it when necessary.

'Come on then,' Lord Honington demanded. 'Hand it over.'

'What for? I don't understand.'

Lord Harry shrugged.

'No. You wouldn't, would you?'

Reluctantly Robert took the mobile phone out of his pocket. But before doing as he was told, he asked: 'You aren't going to break it are you?'

'I hope not.'

'What do you mean .. hope not?'

This conversation was getting too much for Rita who had realised exactly what needed to be done.

'For goodness sake give it to him before that helicopter homes in on it with one of its missiles!' she cried, grabbing it out of his hand and passing it over as directed.

For the umpteenth time since meeting these unbelievable people Robert was flabbergasted again. His next words told them why.

'Be careful with that. It's not just any old mobile. Those are real diamonds encrusted on it. Goodness knows what it cost, but Grace bought it for me. If she does ever speak to me again I would hate it to be to explain what had happened to it.'

Lord Honington gave him a sympathetic look.

'I'm sorry,' he explained. 'But while this phone is on board with us we are in danger of capture.'

'No!' Robert cried out in desperation. He dived towards Lord Harry, trying to snatch the precious gift out of his grasp, but he was unsuccessful, almost toppling over the side of the swaying basket as the phone dropped downwards. What poor Robert didn't see was the pilot of the balloon directly below them catch it and put it into his own pocket.

Meanwhile Lord Honington sought to allay Robert's fears.

'Don't worry my boy. Fred Barnes caught it and one day I'm sure he will be able to return it to you.'

Robert grabbed the side of the basket, hauled himself to his feet and looked over. The man below, who was obviously the aforementioned Fred Barnes, looked up, tapped his pocket and gave him the thumbs-up sign. Then as the gaggle of balloons rounded the sharp side of a rocky tor, momentarily moving out of sight of the chasing Apache, Fred gave them a cheerful wave as he swooped away towards the ground. The helicopter reappeared, hovered for a few seconds and dived down after him.

'Right!' shouted the noble lord as they drifted round another bluff. 'Now's our chance.'

And they floated out of sight of the helicopter and the posse trying unsuccessfully to follow them on the ground. The steep rocky sides of the ravine appeared almost certain to rip the canopy to shreds, but Lord Harry was a much too accomplished balloonist to let that happen. He steered a course right through the middle of it, rounding a bend as the rest of the group disappeared in a graceful group along a safe looking valley, followed soon afterwards by a very fast moving helicopter.

So while Lord Honington set a somewhat roundabout course for Blackpool, the rest of the unlikely airborne procession headed in the opposite direction.

The perfect solution, thought Hella.

'How can we get all the way to the coast without being detected?' Robert worried.

'We can't. But time is now our big advantage,' Rita reassured him.

'And when we get there what will happen?'

Who knows indeed, worried Robert, but said no more.

Meanwhile the noble lord has his own problems trying to avoid sharp rocks protruding from the precipices on either side of them while maintaining enough height to soar up into the sky again at the end of the gorge which acted like a wind tunnel buffeting them along precariously before blasting them out into the fresh air. Thermals were the key and boy, did they do a good job. The balloon and its occupants were launched upwards like a rocket from Cape Kennedy soaring to the stars.

Through all this Lord Harry somehow managed to keep his control and composure of the violently bucking craft. Otherwise they could all have been flung out of the basket like so much laundry blown in the wind without a washing line to hang on.

As it turned out they did survive and it wasn't until the sausage balloon was sedately floating along above the M55, Blackpool's main approach road, that the police car and other pursuit vehicles appeared racing to keep up with them. Fortunately the helicopter was still nowhere in sight although the pilot must have been informed of his error by then.

When he saw the posse back on their tail Lord Harry let out an exhilarating bellow of sheer joy.

'What a fantastic day!' he cried, beaming like a victory beacon. 'I've not had as much fun in years!'

'You and me too,' muttered Robert ironically as he huddled in a corner of the basket shaking with a mixture of terror and frustration.

'What now?' asked Rita.

'I shudder to think,' Hella chuckled in between striving to keep calm herself while allaying Robert's convulsions.

'Now the real thrills begin!' Lord Harry chimed in. 'Hang on to whatever you can! We're going in!'

With that he swung the balloon onto a course to the south of the Pleasure Beach past the Stargate through the sand dunes. About fifty yards out to sea they turned to run parallel to the shore, sailing nearer and nearer to the top resorts famous rolling waves. The basket was scraping the crests when Lord Honington suddenly shouted: 'Right! Now is the time! Jump!'

His three passengers just stood there. Not quite sure what was required of them, as if they needed further encouragement. But they did and the noble lord was the man to do it.

'Go on!' he urged. 'The speed boat will pick you up. Now!'

This sparked Rita, ever the daredevil to follow his orders. She took two steps them threw herself out of the basket. Hella followed, eyes tightly closed as she did so.

But Robert remained frozen to the spot.

'Come on,' said Lord Harry, extending a hand towards him. But at that moment the basket bounced off a breaker, hurling the balloonist into thin air, but only sending Robert sprawling flat on his face on the floor.

The sudden loss of human ballast sent the giant sausage soaring into the air, which was rather fortunate as it just cleared the end of the South Pier as it careered off in a violently unstable flight. Higher and higher missing the Central Pier's Big Wheel by inches and blown onwards and upwards straight for the famous Blackpool Tower. All that Robert could see as it flew directly at the giant metal landmark was an imminent collision with the Meccano-like structure. Kneeling near the side of the basket face at eye level on the edge he braced himself for what this time must be the end!

But at the last minute his strength gave out. He slumped into a heap in the bottom corner of the basket awaiting the inevitable. But it certainly didn't happen as expected.

First there was a judder which rocked the basket so violently that Robert was thrown across into the opposite corner, cracking his head on one of the metal frames. Dazed, he was then aware of whirling around as if on a fairground ride and finally crashing to an abrupt halt against something extremely hard. The basket gave one more almighty judder before becoming ominously distorted.

Unsure whether or not to move, he blinked an eye upwards and saw that the deflated canopy had snagged on a jagged part of the tower, then wrapped itself around the narrowest stretch of the structure leaving it suspended against some of the bulkier spars.

A precarious position indeed!

But what could he do? He was afraid to move in case it made his position worse and well aware that if he didn't the situation could get even more dangerous without his help. The current crop of creaks and groans, ripping noises combined to make the second option even more imminent.

Before he could make up his mind, however, there was a sudden snap and the whole contraption slid thirty or so feet towards the ground. Fortunately it was brought to a juddering halt by another snag against the tower which brought Robert into very tentative action. Somehow he managed to inch himself into a position from where he could get a good idea what was happening. Up above he could see the canopy start to tear again, slipping apart and causing another fall. Once more it was only a matter of time until the process repeated itself. But afterwards he could just make out crowd gathering on the promenade below. The best news though was that the roof of the main Tower building was now within reach if he had the courage to jump for it.

Further threatening sounds made up his mind for him and an instant before the balloon and its basket plummeted to the ground sending people scattering everywhere to try to escape, he leapt out of it.

CHAPTER 11

Seconds later Robert did in fact land on the Tower ballroom roof, a covering long in need of repair, which leaked copiously onto the dance floor whenever it rained. His landing was full of bruises and thankfully no real personal injury. The roof was a different matter. Although it didn't actually collapse, large flakes of gold leaf ceiling decoration did rain down on the waltzers moving gracefully beneath his point of impact. Robert knew nothing of this, of course, while the dancers had no idea what had caused it. They weren't able to see the horde of police officers who invaded the building to the horror or queuers at the box office.

Naturally the fugitive on the roof had much more pressing matters on his mind. How to get off the top of the old building and into the relative safety of the interior.

Ten yards away across the precarious looking surface a half open door beckoned. What to do? Robert's mind was made up for him by a sound he dreaded. The beat of helicopter rotors from the opposite side of the Tower. No time to think. He raced across to the door, closed it behind him and nearly fell headlong down a flight of steps leading down into darkness from beyond which the unmistakable sound of Blackpool's world famous Wurlitzer organ filled the air.

Outside the helicopter emerged from behind the building just too late to see the door close behind the pilot's target. So it continued sweeping the whole area as best it could.

Meanwhile Robert stumbled down the stairs and through a door leading to the shadowy corridor behind the 'Gods', the top tier seats looking down onto the dance floor below which had been cleared because of the debris falling from the ceiling. He glanced up to see that a number of gaps had appeared in the classic paintings of angels, cherubs and artistically clad humanoid figures. At the other end of the ballroom the organist continued to soldier on through his repertoire of dance tunes.

Robert was pleased to see no sign of pursuit yet but was sure it would come. His best chance of escape seemed to be to get down and mingle with the crowds of would-be-dancers gathered around the edges of the floor wondering what on earth was going on? He wasn't exactly dressed for a rumba, but his ballooning gear was enough to enable him to pass himself off as a maintenance man. Not that he was going to hang around long enough to help out, but at least it would make his progress towards one of the exits that much easier.

Bludgeoning through the elegantly dressed patrons, he forced his way out through the double doors into a plush carpeted reception area. Unfortunately he could hear agitated voices and pounding feet heading his way from round a corner so his only way out was down another flight of stairs to the next level. There he rounded a corner to be faced with a dead end – at least that's what it would have been had it not harboured the ghoulishly gaudy entrance to the world-famous Count Dracula exhibition.

'How long does it take to get through?' he asked the white faced beauty in the dangerously low cut dress behind the till.

'As long as it takes,' she pouted, leaning forward to give him the kind of view of her anatomy that would have horrified him before the onslaught of this incredibly out of character escapade, but now served to increase the alien lust coursing through his veins.

'Watch out for vampires,' she called after him as he stepped into the absolute blackness of the exhibition.

'I will,' he replied hopefully, dodging the door which closed quickly behind him. Even before his current adventures he had lusted after the voluptuous female bloodsuckers on television and at the cinemas.

Now, however, he wasn't so sure. But that was ridiculous. This was a virtual fairground attraction. Real vampires wouldn't be found dead in here. Except in the movies of course. And they weren't real anyway. Were they?

In an instant his earlier hopes and fears appeared to have been realised! A blinding flash of lightning, artificial he presumed, split the darkness to reveal a Dracula-like figure, black cloak and all, sucking blood from the exposed neck of a beautiful young woman wearing only a pure white full-length nightie.

But what terrified him most of all about this man-made diorama was when the girl's eyes, which had been tightly closed, burst wide open and stared directly into his!

Then the whole scene vanished back into absolute darkness leaving Robert trying frantically to regain his composure for the umpteenth time that day; or night depending in which frantic fantasy he was standing at any particular time.

No sooner had he done so than there was the sound of a door being flung open somewhere followed by the thumping of heavy boots along the exhibition floor.

'Don't worry. If he's in here we'll find him. And he can't get out because we've got the entrance and exit covered.'

The officer had hardly finished speaking when Robert stepped right into another horrific situation.

Lightning flashed again and there she was directly blocking his path and beckoning to him – the voluptuous vampire from that awful diorama!

'Come. Come with me,' she urged, her eyes compelling him to move closer. But as her fangs bared Robert shrank back.

More lightning and an ominous rumble of thunder as she hissed again: 'Follow me. It's your only chance.'

Darkness returned with more thunder in the background. Or was it the rumble of heavy boots?

'Quick!' came a voice from around the corner. 'Follow that lightning. He must have triggered it!'

Then in sheer frustration as a knee banged against a sharp object: 'Bloody hell! Can't somebody put the flaming lights on?'

Robert was still caught in two minds groping in the dark when he felt a hand gripping his arm.

'Wake up. I'm not a vampire,' she urged. 'Lord Honington sent me!'

Displaying at least the strength of a vampire she dragged him to a side door which would have been almost invisible to anyone who did not know it was. The door opened and he was shoved through it into a partially lit passage. His vampirical friend floated in beside him, closing it as quietly as she could. Robert was about to speak, but she put her fingers to her lips to silence him. A moment later the heavy boots went clomping by inside the exhibition. When they had faded into the persistent darkness the vampire removed her false fangs and gave him the most charming smile.

'Lord Honington is one of our major shareholders,' she explained. 'He asked us to get you out of here, but we didn't realise how difficult it was going to be. You're a really wanted man. Trail of destruction and all that.'

'So are you going to turn me in then?'

The girl smiled even more warmly.

'Don't be silly! Lord Honington would never forgive me. But you will have to face a couple of hair-raising experiences.'

'As if I haven't done already!' laughed Robert. ';Lead on my dear and let's get it over with. What's your name by the way?'

'Elvira,' she replied.

'I might have known,' said Robert.

They both chuckled at this and became more relaxed with each other. Robert thought how attractive she was without those vicious fangs. Elvira noticed and told him: 'I know what you're thinking, but you should always remember one thing about vampires: their bite is always worse than their bark.'

Again they both laughed and she led him through another door into what he couldn't fail to recognise as backstage at the famous Blackpool Tower Circus. All around him were clowns, acrobats, glamorously dressed showgirls and over near the entrance to the ring, a rider on a stationary motor bike revving it up like mad as if raring to go. Resting on the pillion was a crash helmet.

'Put it on and get on behind him,' Elvira shouted above the noise and hang on to him for dear life!'

Robert had no choice but to do as she said and no sooner was he in position arms round the rider, the engine roared even louder. In a flash they entered the ring at high speed, launching into a huge tilted wooden barrel which bore the words 'Wall of Death – Abandon Hope All Ye Who Enter Here!'

All around them the audience went crazy with excitement. The rider let out a great whoop of delight while Robert did the only thing possible in the circumstances. Hung on for grim death while praying frantically that the centrifugal force would keep them from crashing to the bottom of the barrel with the most devastating effect. Round and round inside the barrel they went, higher when they speeded up, lower when they slowed down. Another bike appeared criss-crossing their path with the tiniest margins for error, making figures of eight which almost produced head-on collisions and blowing Robert's mind clear out of his head. Then just as he thought he could bear it no longer the ordeal was over and they raced out into the backstage area without stopping, narrowly missing a group of police officers on the way. Rough riding down two flights of unyielding stairs straight towards a pair of double doors flung open by terrified stewards and out into the street, scattering dozens of shocked holidaymakers, as they did so. Still their speed didn't let up. Their wild ride swerved across two lanes of traffic about to move away from the lights, bumped up one side of the kerb and down the other narrowly missing a trundling tram and frightening more people along the promenade en route to the North Pier. A long the side of the amusement arcade at the entrance, through an 'S' bend and out to sea. No-one needed telling to get out of the way. The sight and sound of the hurtling motor cycle was enough. At the end of the pier behind the theatre the rider skidded the machine to a shuddering halt.

'Right!' he yelled. 'Over the rails now!'

Not for the first time in this nightmare escape Robert was stunned into inaction. His driver had no such inhibitions. Mind you he wasn't the one being forced to leap fully clothed into a churning Irish Sea.

'Go on! Get the hell out of here before the cops arrive!'

Robert looked back to where the police were already driving on to the pier hooters hooting, sirens wailing. But before he could decide what to do he was suddenly lifted off his feet, held high over the edge and hurled thirty feet down into the crashing waves. He didn't even have time to hear the motorbike roar off back along the pier causing to swerve precariously into various stalls and gift shops and cafés. Seconds later the rider had disappeared into the maze of back-streets. Later the Wall of Death riders would all be interviewed by the police but the verdict would be 'Aided and abetted by person or persons unknown.'

Circus performers are a notoriously close-knit loyal community and those in the Tower Circus cast were no exceptions.

CHAPTER 12

The unfortunate Robert hit the sea hard, so much so that he was stunned and began to sink to what would have been death by drowning. Spluttering and thrashing about he was about to go down for the third time when the sound of whirring propellers and a pair of strong hands hauled him out to safety. Seconds later he was flapping around on the bottom of a rescue dinghy with alternate shoves in the chest and exhalations of foul sea water.

'He'll be OK,' said a familiar voice. 'We got him out just in time.'

'We'll have to get him out of those clothes or he will catch his death,' came a reply.

They were of course Lord Harry and Rita, not the police as he had first feared. Robert was just beginning to relax in their care but then he was hit with another bombshell.

'In that case we'll get him to the sub as soon as possible. Then you two girls can have your wicked way with him.'

This startled Robert wide awake again and absolutely horrified. It wasn't so much the thought of Rita and Hella doing what they would with him, but the little three-letter word that had slipped out of the noble lord's mouth with such apparent harmlessness but really such menace.

Sub! Submarine! Claustrophobia! Robert tried to sit up and protest, but a stabbing pain in the head and sheer mental exhaustion sent him flopping back down again. His two rescuers carried on regardless, but Robert began to blubber and shake all over again.

'Oh no! He's having a relapse!' cried Rita, preparing to give him more resuscitation.

But before she could do so Lord Honington stopped her.

'Listen my dear. I know you are anxious to give him mouth to mouth when we get him onto the sub. The best thing at the moment is to rendezvous as soon as possible; before they send the coastguard out after us. We're in enough trouble already without having the authorities investigating the fact that we have a former Royal Navy submarine lurking so close to Britain's number one holiday resort.' With that he turned up the throttle and sent the dinghy storming out to sea at an alarming rate.

As for Robert, he had never found his sea legs even on the expensive cruises Grace had forced him to endure. Now he was being taken to one of his worst nightmares on board a submarine!

Back on the pier everything was confused and frustrated. Police and personal posse running in all directions, unable to continue the chase. Mobiles in a cacophony of ring tones and 'allo's. All seeking vessels to hunt down the fugitives. The trouble was that in truth nobody was getting anywhere.

One policewoman got so carried away by it all that she perched on the second rung of the safety railings, like Kate Winslet on the Titanic, let go with both hands gesticulating frantically. Unfortunately she lost her balance and plummeted thirty feet into the choppy sea beneath the pier. A gallant male colleague risked his own life diving in fully clothed to save her from drowning. Both of them ended up perched on a narrow horizontal girder being bombarded with crashing waves as if someone was hurling buckets of water into their faces every few seconds. This added to the time lost in pursuing the fugitives as the drenched duo would have to be picked up by the first boat to arrive and taken to the shore where an ambulance was waiting to get them to hospital.

None of this was noticed by Lord Honington and his unlikely crew, who were racing to see Robert safely on board the submarine. Mercifully he had lapsed into unconsciousness. This meant that when the sub surfaced and men leapt out of the conning tower to help, despite the dead weight they were not further hampered by his wild struggling to avoid the drop. Unfortunately one of his rescuers slipped on the wet surface and the patient was sent flopping down onto the hard deck below.

The impact went some way to reviving him and he growned: 'What's going on?' before sinking back into oblivion before being hauled away and laid out on one of the vessel's hospital bunks.

'Thank heavens it's not a hammock!' chuckled Rita as she and Hella arrived to try to revive him.

'He would probably end up getting so tangled up he would throttle himself,' laughed Hella.

There was a short hesitation before Rita gave her friend a nudge and urged: Go on then. Do what you've been wanting to do all along.'

'What?' said Hella.

'You know very well what I mean. Give him the kiss of life you daft bat.'

Needing no further pushing Hella did what she had wanted to do for a long time. It was the kiss of life for it brought Robert back to full alert in an instant.

'What the hell! Grace! Stop it! Oh my God! It's you!'

Hella staggered back no sure whether to laugh or cry. But Robert realised his mistake immediately and was mortified.

Now wide awake he tried desperately to sit up, protesting: 'No! No! That's not what I meant.'

In her heart of hearts Hella knew exactly what he meant and the effects of that kiss had at the very least given them both real prospects of a new lease of life.

But before she could reply they were interrupted by Lord Harry.

'Hope I'm not intruding,' he said. 'Just wanted to ask how you are feeling?'

The question was clearly directed at Robert, who tried to reassure their benefactor by saying he was all right. He obviously wasn't but appeared to be getting back to as normal as he could ever be in the circumstances.

Honington seemed to accept this and continued: 'Good, because we really need to get this sub hidden as soon as possible. Otherwise things could get quite dangerous.'

'Not that dangerous surely,' Rita observed.

'Would depth charges be deadly enough for you my dear?'

Even though his revelation stunned them the noble lord explained: 'You see, not only is this a World War submarine, decommissioned or not, there is another problem ..'

'Don't tell me,' laughed Rita, tongue in cheek. 'It's a U-boat!'

'Exactly. You are so perceptive my dear and destroyers will already be on the way here. So we must keep one step ahead of them.'

'They wouldn't really depth charge us would they?' Robert sounded as if that was what he hoped, but knowing what had happened so far he couldn't be sure.

Lord Harry sought to reassure him especially in light of what was to come if and when the sub reached its destination.

'They would have to locate us first lad and that won't happen if I have anything to do with it.'

As if to emphasise his words the sub juddered to a higher speed the periscope went up and Honington looked through the binocular lens.

'Ah. Quite a flotilla. We'd better run deeper. Don't want them to anticipate our course,' he said.

'And what is our destination?' Robert wanted to know.

'You'll find out soon enough my boy.'

'Isle of Man,' Rita cut in. 'It's the only place. But it's so small surely there's no where to hide.'

But Hella didn't agree.

'If Lord Harry is taking us up to the Isle of Man he must have good reason to do so.'

The noble lord seemed highly delighted to receive this vote of confidence from such a beautiful girl.

'Quite correct my dear. We are going somewhere on, or should I say under, one of the island's most unfathomable mysteries.'

'Which is?' asked Rita.

'The Chasms. Part of the coastline near the village of Craigneish where the cliffs have split from top to bottom like a pack of cards. The legend has it that the resultant fissures are bottomless but I can tell you they are not. For the rest of it I shall let you find out for yourselves. Before then however, I have to tell you there are some daunting challenges to be faced and I know you will be up to them.'

'Now why on earth should I think those words are meant specifically for me?' Robert groaned.

Lord Honington put his hand gently on Robert's shoulder.

CHAPTER 12

'Because it's true, my boy and I am sure you will once again face up to those challenges.'

Robert smiled ironically.

'Go on then. Tell me the worst.'

'Scuba. Does that word mean anything to you? Have you ever been scuba diving?'

Before he could add anything Robert burst into a torrent of panic.

'Oh no! No, no, no, no, no, no! I can't! I won't! You can't make me! No! Dion't tell me. There's no other way. All right then, But at least have the decency to tell me … why?'

There was no mistaking the relief in Lord Harry's expression. He knew that once again Robert would do what had to be done although it was something totally alien to him.

It's the only way I'm afraid. There is a large cavern beneath the Chasms which is half full of water. Unfortunately the entrance is too narrow and the rocks on either side too jagged for the submarine to get through safely allowing you to disembark above the water line. Therefore the only way is to use scuba equipment getting off the boat and onto the dry rocky platform. It's only a short swim if you know what you are doing.'

'And if you don't, how far?' Robert demanded.

'About a hundred yards,' Lord Harry replied somewhat tentatively. 'But we have fully trained crew members to guide you and give support where necessary.'

Hella put her arm around the hapless Robert and said: 'My hero. I know you'll do it.'

As always, of course, Robert had no real choice in the matter. It was difficult to overcome his claustrophobia in the submarine, let alone wearing a mask and swimming under water. But he had to do it and when the vessel eased its way into the mouth of the cave he was ready and almost willing even if unable to get his gear on.

Lord Honington and the girls accomplished this with little trouble. In fact Rita and Hella were quite excited at the prospect.. Both had done scuba diving before but not in the confines of such a rocky cavern. The noble lord, however, didn't want to waste any time unnecessarily on the dry granite platform changing back into their dry everyday clothes which had been brought across in waterproof bags.

As they did so Hella looked up at the soaring fissures which seared up through the cliffs. At the top a tiny split of blue sky beckoned.

'They really are high,' she said. 'You weren't exaggerating were you?'

Still on board the sub Robert was having trouble getting into his scuba outfit. Never having been in diving equipment before he found the wet suit almost impossible to adapt to. First the legs stuck to his legs like a bicycle puncture repair outfit. After a superhuman effort his helpers, who could hardly contain their laughter, ensured a close but comfortable fit and then it was the turn of the arms and the rest of the body with similar problems. Then trio mask and air pipe. Having apparently put them on successfully Robert started to splutter and choke as if he were being asphyxiated. Just as he looked likely to collapse completely one of his helpers tapped on his face mask and shouted: 'You don't have to hold your breath you know. That's what the gear is for. Breathe goddamnit!'

So saying he slapped the reluctant diver on the back with a dramatic effect.

Poor Robert staggered forward, clutched his hands to his throat and crashed around almost upskittling a table. But then he got himself together, gasping: 'Come of then. Let's get on with it.'

'Right sir,' smiled the helpful rating. 'And may I say it takes some courage to do what you are doing never having been under water like this before.'

'Yes, but I'm afraid there is one important item we appear to have overlooked. Well two actually.'

'And that it?'

'Flippers!'

'Flippers? Ah. And they are a must.'

"fraid so.'

So as there was no alternative and after a session of flip flopping in all directions and toppling head-first onto the deck Robert managed to stagger into the air lock and await his watery fate. Water filled the chamber all around him, but somehow he managed to remain calm enough to launch himself out into the cold water where another diver took hold of his hand and towed him to the surface. After another session of spluttering and considerable shivers, Lord Honington and the girls hauled him up onto the rocky outcrop where he floundered around until they got him out of the scuba outfit and into his own clothing.

'There you go!' Rita chuckled.

Lord Honington said nothing but beamed a smile of relief, while Hella was so overcome with joy that she flung her arms around the flounderer and gave him the most amazing kiss of his life.

This was yet another shock for Robert, who was used to the more formal embraces from a fiancée with solid English reticence in such matters. Even on her wedding night Grace would be loath to allow herself the luxury of such passion.

But what caught Robert's eye in equal surprise was the way Hella appeared to be similarly unsettled as she staggered away in bewilderment.

Robert flopped onto his back like the proverbial fish out of water, eyes closed, body totally slumped as if in a stupor.

There was a short silence as if nobody knew quite what to say. Lord Harry finally broke it.

'Time to go' he said.

Robert opened one eye then the other, staring up at the roof with its soaring chasms which reached to patches of blue sky at the top of the cliffs.

'Where?' he asked. 'Up there?'

The noble lord helped him to his feet.

'Absolutely right my boy.'

For the umpteenth time Robert was flabbergasted and refused to budge.

'No! Not this time. I've never been mountaineering and I'm not prepared to start now!'

Lord Harry shook his head in the long suffering way he always did when Robert became adamant about things.

'All I can say is that once again you have Hobson's choice,' he pointed out. 'You can either have the courage to climb up one of the chasms, which does present a certain amount of risk. Or you can stay down here and either starve to death, freeze or drown when the tide reaches into the cave in about two hours time, flooding it completely.'

CHAPTER 13

'So that's it then,' scoffed Robert. 'Only choice is no choice. Lead on my lord and we shall follow or die trying.'

Lord Harry smiled in an almost fatherly way. In many ways he admired Robert; a young man torn from his comfort zone and thrust into the most bizarre set of adventures he wouldn't even have imagined possible a few days ago.

Rita also realised how alien their situation must seem to someone of a solid back ground of social conformity.

'That's the spirit!' she added, realising how false her words must have sounded in the circumstances while Hella remained silent looking both bewildered and pensive, her finger lightly touching her lips.

At that point Honington realised just how beautiful she really was. His fantasy was broken by a serious question from Robert.

'So how do you propose that we scale the smooth wet walls of such a chasm?'

'Good question,' smiled Lord Harry. 'But of course you cannot know that we have carved out footholds in one side of the fissure.'

But Robert was not convinced.

'Even so it would take someone with considerable mountaineering skills to make such a climb successfully. It's a pity there are no ropes hanging down from the summit – or even a rope ladder.'

'Not necessary, I assure you my dear boy.'

'Ah. I get it,' Rita intervened. 'The chasm in question must be just wide enough for it to be used to brace our backs against one wall and use the footholds to hutch ourselves upwards. I've seen it on the telly.'

'Seeing it on TV doesn't mean necessarily that anyone can just up and do it.' Robert remarked, still unsure about the way Hella was looking at him.

But as Honington had already pointed out there was no alternative and preparations for the climb began.

'I shall go first and there will be ropes linking us all tied to me.'

The noble lord gave them all a demonstration of how to complete the ascent pushing his back against the wall and using the footholds as he had explained. Hella was to go next followed by Robert and then Rita who was to help him if he got into trouble.

'Progress will be arduous but not impossible,' said Lord Harry. 'So the quicker we get there the better. And remember: whatever you do, don't look down.'

He made sure that his gaze lingered pointedly on Robert, who said nothing but wore an embarrassed expression which said it all.

Slowly, painstakingly and ultimately successfully they began to inch up into the chasm. Lord Harry and the girls actually appeared to enjoy the adventure. Robert wasn't so sure but at least obeyed their leader's warning to keep his gaze level or upwards. It wasn't easy as the temptation to look down was overwhelming. At first the process was easy but the longer they climbed the more tiring it became. For every yard of progress they made two more seemed to be added towards the top. Robert battled on bravely and was quite proud of himself until Rita, in an effort to spur him on, told him how well he was doing.

Unfortunately the automatic reaction was to look down and thank her.

Which was what he did, with near disastrous results! It took only a glance, but then vertigo kicked in and he simply froze. Mercifully that was better than what might have happened, for if he had panicked spasmodically he might have lost his footing and dragged them all down with him to what would have been serious injury on impact or even death. As it was Lord Harry tightened his grip on the safety line, bracing himself against all eventualities while Rita inched herself into a position whereby she might be able to ease Robert out of his panic inflicted paralysis.

Meanwhile Hella remained as still as she could so as not to cause any further danger.

'It's all right now, my boy,' said Honington. 'We'll get you back on the climb again.'

By now Rita had managed to settle as near as possible to their stricken colleague and began to soothe him with a series of caresses. Gradually Robert's panic subsided and he moved slowly into a less cramped position, looking up at both Lord Harry and Hella.

'There you go. Nothing to worry about now,' Murmured Rita.

'Sorry,' gasped Robert. 'Won't happen again I promise.'

With a superhuman effort he began the ascent again and the tension dropped from critical back to tense.

'Well done Robert,' said the noble lord. 'Took some courage not to lose it altogether in that situation.'

The girls agreed but Robert reserved judgement until they had all reached safety of a ledge about eighty feet from the chasm's summit. Relief was rife among them but Hella was the Devil's advocate this time.

'So when do we start the second part of the climb?'

But in reply Lord Harry sprang another of his surprises.

'We don't.'

'What do you mean?' Robert wanted to know, his voice filled with new dread.

'We go through there,' the noble lord replied, pointing behind them to what looked like the entrance to a cave.

Rita started to say something but Robert interrupted her rather rudely she thought.

'So it's all downhill from now on,' he chuckled ironically.

'Well … not exactly,' was the answer.

'I knew it! So what death-defying feat is next on the list?'

Honington headed into the cave, beckoning them to follow. As they did so Rita immediately realised that there was indeed one major problem.

'How do we get across the other chasms?' she asked. 'I presume that's where we're going. There doesn't seem to be any other way.'

'But it's not just a long dark trek through a claustrophobic cave is it?' said Robert in a tone which seemed to answer his own question.

'I'm afraid it isn't,' replied Lord Harry.

'It's much worse than that, isn't it?'

'I'm afraid it is a little scary. But completely safe and I know you will cope, my boy, as you always do.'

'We'll help all we can,' added Hella.

Once again Robert had to grin and bear it as Lord Harry led them through the entrance to where they were confronted by a contraption that most kids would love to ride, Indiana Jones would have thrived on, but for present company was as daunting as could possibly be.

Every adventure playground has one, the army use them for training purposes and even some pleasure parks have begun to feature them. Wire fixed slightly higher at one end than the other so that pulleys run along it smoothly enough to haul a hanging seat with a safety belt so that a person can slide down the length of it being pulled to a stop by an operator holding a safety cable at the top.

'Pretty basic isn't it?' Lord Harry commented. 'But quite safe I assure you.'

'It will be perfectly safe for me because I won't be using the thing,' Robert cut in.

But the noble lord shook his head rather ruefully.

'Sorry, but you really have no choice.'

'What do you mean?' You can't make me do anything I don't want to,' Robert said indignantly.

'True. But in this case there is no other way.'

'Why it that?'

'Because the high wire is the only way to go. Even if you were able to climb back down into the cavern you would discover there is no way out. Which is why the sub had to get us as near as possible. The underwater cave contains currents and with the U-boat gone there would be nobody else to help you.'

'What about climbing to the top of the chasm?' Rita suggested.

'Another no-no,' Lord Harry replied. 'the fissure is too wide to do what we did to get here and the walls too smooth and sheer to scale.'

'So once again I'm stuck with it,' said Robert.

'I'm afraid so.'

CHAPTER 13

The unfortunate Robert shrugged his shoulders becoming resigned to his fate once again.

'We'd better get on with it then, I can't promise anything, but I'll just do my best not to let you down.'

'You won't let us down,' Hella smiled. 'You haven't done so far and I know you won't this time. We have every confidence in you. Why don't you have some in yourself?'

In a sudden movement which caught them all off-guard Robert leant across, put his arms around Hella and gave her a kiss that made their earlier one seem like a peck on the cheek. She was so stunned she actually fell backwards into Rita's waiting arms totally out of reality.

'Well, well,' laughed Lord Honington. 'At last it looks like we're beginning to see the real man in you.'

'Never mind that. Let's get on with it as I said. Shall I go first?' Robert urged.

But despite being taken aback by the new Robert, Lord Harry put up his hand.

'No. I don't think that would be wise. Although I need to stay here and control the safety line it would be best if Rita went first to make sure all is well at the other end.'

So it was that the daredevil stunt pilot was strapped into the harness and launched into the dark recesses of the lower cave. All went well and the noble lord hauled the contraption back up for Hella to go next.

Her transit passed without incident and the time came for Robert to join them. Lord Harry hooked the line behind them and helped his friend into the harness not without some difficulty.

Then they were ready and keeping a tight rein on the safety line Honington sent Robert on his way, albeit at a slower pace than the two girls had done.

For his part the intrepid passenger tried to keep his eyes tightly closed while hanging on grimly. But he couldn't resist the odd glimpse of the apparently bottomless chasms as he passed over them. Then, after and endless seeming flight he swung gently into the waiting arms of the two girls, who helped him to dismount and onto solid ground where he shook a little while regaining his composure.

Lord Harry's decent was altogether more difficult. He had to manoeuvre the safety line round a geared pulley system playing it out to maintain his progress at the correct speed. But all went well and eventually he joined his friends on the ground floor as it were.

'I can't say it will be all downhill from now,' he told them. 'But I can say that although you are in for the surprise of your lives you will all be pleased to know that there are to be no more nasty shocks in store.'

This particularly pleased Robert who had fallen into step beside Hella while Rita had joined the noble lord up front. All four had been given torches to ensure there were no unfortunate trip-ups on the rough cavern floor.

'How far do we have to go now?' asked Robert.

'Far enough but not too far,' Lord Harry replied. 'And I assure you that in the end every step will have been worthwhile.'

One of the most amazing things which caught Rita's eye was the fact that, unlike most if not all of the caves she had been in, this one showed no sign of moisture seeping through.

'Is it an artificial tunnel?' she wanted to know.

But Lord Honington was keeping all information to himself.

'Soon enough,' he said. 'All will be revealed in good time.'

Although they were hundreds of feet below the surface by this time, Robert was surprised that the air was so fresh, which helped to ease the claustrophobic effect of the tunnel, which had no other passages leading off it.

The way led up a short rise, over the brow of the hill and downwards for at least one hundred yards to where a strong metal door barred the way.

Robert's misgivings returned immediately.

Why was such a strong door necessary?

What lay behind it?

What new shock did the noble lord have up his sleeve for them?

He was soon to find out.

Without another word Lord Harry pressed a sequence of buttons on the right-hand side of the door, which swung open to reveal a black hole of seemingly impenetrable blackness.

CHAPTER 13

'Follow me my friends,' he invited them, stepping through and flicking a succession of switches with the kind of flourish that only someone with complete confidence can display.

As usual the intrepid trio did as they were instructed and walked into the most awe-inspiring experience imaginable!

CHAPTER 14

The scene before them was like something from a blockbuster James Bond movie. A vast floodlit cavern containing three heavy duty helicopters clustered around a grating which covered what appeared to be a manhole. The choppers in turn were surrounded by maintenance and refuelling equipment although there was no sign of anyone working on the machines which made sure the whole place had been in total darkness when they arrived.

Other workshop machines and computer consoles nestled around the cave's perimeter, the most impressive to their left just inside the door. The focus of this one was a large red button which seemed to have ominous implications for all of them. Next to what Robert was already calling 'The Doomsday Button' was a stainless steel lever. The temptation to pull it back and then press the red button was almost overwhelming but for once his instincts told him the truth.

Lord Harry would do it for him soon enough! Without a word he leaned across and pushed the steel lever forward.

Both Robert and Rita took a step towards him but the noble lord held up his hand.

'Calm down my dears. I just activated our escape route.'

But Robert could not bear the suspense any longer.

'Escape from what?'

'Yes,' said Rita ominously. 'Tell us before I am forced to make you.'

Although Robert had never witnessed Rita actually indulge herself in violence he could well imagine she was capable of it in extreme circumstances and their present dilemma was beginning to fall into that category.

'The complete destruction of this island,' explained Lord Harry, then added quickly as shock turned to anger on his two protagonists faces:

CHAPTER 14

'If and when I depress that red button. But before doing that I would like you to give me the opportunity to let you know why.'

For a moment nothing happened, no one moved. The large sliding doors on the far side of the cavern rolled open and a white van, police car plus several other vehicles drove in stopping just short of the three helicopters.

At the same time the domed roof began to open slowly from the centre like a segmented camera shutter set for time exposure.

Robert was already becoming apprehensive and this mood was heightened considerably by the sight of the people alighting.

First out of the Rolls Royce was Lord Honington's effete partner Henry.

'Stop!' he cried much more forcefully than might have been expected of a man with such a disposition. 'Don't move! Don't move or I shall shoot!'

He needn't have worried as they all remained frozen at the sight of the huge service revolver he was waving about like a madman. All except Hella of course, who had remained speechless since their entry into this amazing place. She drew closer to Robert, hugging him tightly to stop him fainting away on the spot.

Poor Robert! His horror was becoming even more unbearable as first Hella's manic partner, then Grace followed by the motel security man, Rita's husband and a whole gaggle of mobile policemen, joined Henry under the increasingly opening roof. Faced by such overwhelming odds Robert was spurred into one final act of helpless courage.

'Look! It's me you all want. I caused all this trouble. Take me and let the other three go. All they have done is help me. They haven't committed any crime.'

Ironically it wasn't Harry or the police who replied. Not even Rita's husband or Hella's rampant partner. It was Grace; a new Grace full of sympathy and concern.

'Oh Robert. You poor innocent fool. I knew you were naïve but not quite as much as you really are.'

Not for the first time in recent days Robert was once again flabbergasted. Grace showing him compassion, not demeaning or belittling him as she usually did. The world really had gone crazy and him with it.

But she wasn't so caring and gentle towards Lord Honington as her next words revealed. Much more like the gruff Grace whom Robert knew so well and loved.

Or did he? As Hella snuggled even closer doubts crept into his befuddled mind. There was no time for further thoughts, however, as she was already berating the not so noble lord as she put it.

'Go on you old hypocrite. Tell him what I've been told during this ridiculous escapade.'

But although rocked by the unwelcome turn of events and seething beneath the surface, Lord Harry kept his composure and replied: 'If you'll let me get a word in edgeways I shall be only too pleased to explain.'

There was a disbelieving silence but it allowed Lord Harry to reveal all.

'Thanks to my dear friend and companion turned traitor the deceptively lovable Henry some of you will know most of it already. But for the benefit of those who don't these are my intentions good or bad, whatever you might think.'

'Get on with it!' Henry shouted. 'The sooner this is over the better!'

The reply was even more condescending than before.

'Don't be so impatient my dear boy. It doesn't become you. As I said: all will become clear soon enough.'

There was a sudden combined movement from across the cavern, but Lord Honington held up his hand which now contained what appeared to be a red remote control.

'Wait!' he ordered. 'As you can see I don't even need to reach that button now.'

Everyone paused and at last he answered their questions.

'I simply intend to sink the Isle of Man.'

Shock and disbelief stunned those listeners who hadn't heard this previously while those who had simply didn't know what to say.

Robert was indeed one of the former group and was first to react.

'You can't do that!' he cried. 'What about all the people who live there?'

Lord Honington shrugged.

'If they haven't the wits to escape they'll go down with it.'

Robert made to attack him, but Hella restrained the once reserved but now much more impetuous character.

'Let it lie. He'll never do it,' she insisted.

'I wouldn't put anything past him,' Rita cut in. 'He's obviously insane,.'

But Lord Harry was adamant.

'I may be insane but I have very good reason for what I'm about to do.'

'Murder some 70 000 people,' shouted Henry. 'How can you justify that?'

'They should have thought of that before stealing my birthright. You know my dear Henry that the English crown's claim for ownership of the Isle Man is invalid. The title to sovereignty of this ancient island belongs to my own family. We are Vikings and proud of it. My ancestors founded the Tynwald, the oldest unbroken system of government, which still works perfectly today. Why should I have to justify anything?'

'But those individuals haven't done enough to die,' said Rita.

'Quite so. Which is why we have done a widespread leaflet drop over the whole island while you have been on the run. They've been given every opportunity to escape and if they choose not to be it on their own heads.'

'No way will we let you get away with it,' cried Rita.

'You have no choice I'm afraid,' Lord Honington retorted.

At which point Robert decided to take matters into his own hands.

'Well I do!' he raged and hurled himself headlong at the evil peer, who neatly side-stepped sending him crashing into the wall. Hella immediately flung herself not towards Lord Harry but to tend the brave but unfortunate Robert who collapsed in a heap clutching his head. As she sobbed over him trying to provide some form of comfort their tormentor simply laughed.

'Maybe that will knock some sense into him,' he chuckled.

While his attention was diverted Rita made her attack but ran straight into a pile driver of a left hook which left her motionless on the floor. But she did manage to knock the remote out of his hand and it shattered beside her still form.

Her irate husband cried out and began to move towards them ominously. But before they could even get more than a few yards the ignoble lord stepped back a few steps and hit the red button. In an instant the roof which was nearly wide open, ground to a halt, but instead of silence another deep rolling sound started up.

It's source was soon revealed by a circle of darkness as the floor in the centre of the cavern began to recede towards the approaching group of people led by the redoubtable Henry. A gaping hole began to yawn ever larger effectually isolating them from the quartet on the other side. The chasm looked black and deep, but left the three helicopters perched on a pedestal in the middle.

With his immediate opposition temporarily immobilized the ignoble Lord Honington seemed to have regained his composure.

'You didn't let me finish,' he said. 'So I shall continue letting you know what I intend to happen to this historic island.'

Before he could in fact continue, Henry cried out: 'It won't work! Both you and I know that. You're mad!'

The only response at first was a groan from the stricken Robert, a sob from Hella and nothing at all from Rita who lay flat on her face oblivious to the world completely unconscious.

At some less perilous time her husband would have made a light remark about someone having actually shut her up if only for a short period of time.

Suddenly it was Lord Harry's turn again.

'I'm afraid you are wrong my boy. You know as well as I do that the Isle of Man sits on a fragile network of caverns like this one supported by narrow pinnacles of subterranean rock surrounded by a deep lake. An explosive eruption on the bottom will create an underground tsunami which will shatter the infrastructure causing the whole island to submerge.

'Taking all those unfortunate enough to still be here with it,' added the police inspector.

'People who ignore warnings deserve all they get,' Harry replied.

'Even you wouldn't commit mass murder my lord,' his former partner insisted.

'They have only themselves to blame as you you have.'

Even as Lord Honington said this the door through which the posse had entered slid shut. Meanwhile the black hole continued to widen towards them,.

'What about all those people living on the coasts of Ireland, Scotland, England and Wales?' Henry wanted to know.

'What about them?'

'Tsunamis will devastate the resorts there as they radiate outwards from the sinking of the island. Thousands will be killed or rendered homeless. How can you justify that?'

He was desperately playing for time to find a solution to the terrible set of circumstances Lord Honington had set in motion. But the errant peer would have none of it.

'They should have thought of the possible consequences when they stole my birthright.

The chasm yawned ever wider.

'You know as well as I do it wasn't them. In all probability they didn't even know about it. If anyone wronged you it was their ancestors.'

But Lord Harry would have none of it.

'Be quiet! You're simply trying to delay me so that I have to abort the mission. Well it won't work. Once set in motion it cannot be stopped. And now my friends it is time to say goodbye.'

The statement coincided with one of the helicopter pilots starting up his machine. As it began to lift off its pedestal Honington made a sudden dash for the rope ladder hanging from its cargo door.

Unfortunately for him but not everyone else the hapless Robert chose that very moment to try to get to his feet. The result was an accidental but very effective collision which sent the peer sprawling with Robert in his wake.

'You stupid clumsy oaf!' Harry yelled trying to kick himself clear. 'Now look what you've done. I might have known it.'

The helicopter hovered directly above them while the ladder swung to and fro above them. Somehow Honington untangled himself and hauled himself onto the bottom of the ladder. Rung by rung he climbed up it. Robert, whose rude awakening had brought him back to full consciousness, managed to get a hand on the final rung, clinging on for his life, which was all he could do. His extra weight caught the pilot unawares and he almost lost control. The aircraft gave a violent shudder and while Robert's terror gave him insane strength to cling on, Lord Harry wasn't so lucky. As they swung out over the abyss he lost his grip and desperately striving to grab his pursuer's arm, missed and plummeted into the hole with a long drawn out scream. His descent finally ended with a sickening thud as his body bounced off an out-jutting rock, followed by a fatal splash into the water.

Robert's own grip was visibly loosening as this happened. Hella let out an equally loud screech as he lost it, but the pilot managed to swing him to the safety of her outstretched arms and they both crashed to the rock floor where they both lay winded and gasping for breath.

Released from the weight dragging it down, the helicopter soared up through the open roof, disappearing into the cloud grey sky.

Safe at last? No way!

Amid all the confusion everyone except Henry appeared to have forgotten the even greater dangerous situation regarding the Isle of Man itself.

Pointing at the floor, which was still receding and then looking at the dome above beginning to close he cried out: 'His lord-ship may be gone but the danger still remains.'

'How can we prevent it?' Grace wanted to know.

At this point the manic eunuch suddenly produced his giant scimitar and began waving it wilding about.

'Nothing is impossible!' he shouted.

But Grace was still not convinced. Her strictly orthodox outlook on life prevented her form realising what he meant.

'But Lord Honington said the process was irreversible once the red button had been repressed.'

While they were talking the floor rumbled on and the roof continued to close. In the centre the pedestal holding the two other helicopters tilted and they slipped off it crashing down to the water below.

This brought Henry out of what appeared to be a cross between a cataleptic fit and a terror induced coma. Visibly shaken and shaking all over he pointed towards a large metal globe hanging from a boom which began to swing out in an arc from the wall. Although it wasn't within range of the black abyss then it clearly would be when the floor got within range of the wall.

'That's the bomb!' he shouted. 'When the floor is fully open I will drop into the hole and when it reaches the right depth it will detonate causing the devastating tsunami.'

'Surely it won't be powerful enough to do that,' ventured Grace.

'You're mistaken my girl. It's a nuclear device!'

Had their situation been less dire Grace would have told him not to be so patronizing, but the word 'nuclear' brought her to her senses.

'Oh! My God!' she cried.

But before either she or Henry could say another word the eunuch yelled. 'Hey! Lover boy! Catch this!'

So saying he flung his scimitar at Robert who somehow avoided being decapitated by diving to the floor. The scimitar hit the computer console, sending up a shower of sparks and a cloud of electric blue smoke.

Grace moved threateningly towards the eunuch who held up his hand to stop her.

'Oh! Come on will You? If I'd wanted to kill him I would have done. Lover boy knows why I did it, don't you?'

Robert got to his feet, went and picked up the weapon and then realised what he had to do.

'That's it. You're learning fast. When all else fails, use brute force and ignorance.'

Despite his patronizing tone Robert turned towards the console and brought the scimitar crashing down with such power that it not only shattered the dials but also sent the red button spinning towards the edge of eternity for everyone concerned.

With a fervour he had never felt before he continued to smash the scimitar down again and again until the console was no more than a pile of broken rubbish, its wires severed and the power gone.

The weapon's blade finally snapped as had Robert's rabid reserve and the rumble and rattle of machinery was silenced forever.

The threat of extinction for the Isle of Man and its inhabitants was over.

EPILOGUE

Later with everyone safely aboard the rescue helicopter on the way back to the mainland there were a number of issues official and personal to be resolved.

In the absence of any immediate complaints, formal or personal, the police had decided to withhold any charges against anyone until their investigations were complete. They were treating Henry as a witness rather than a suspect and Robert as an unfortunate victim of circumstances albeit a monumental one.

Rita, who had now come round after Lord Harry's KO punch, was in the arms of her husband and as oblivious to what was going on around them as if she were still unconscious.

Grace had just finished a conversation with the eunuch, who was sitting next to her. She turned to Robert on her other side. He tried to hide his cringe against the expected onslaught., But it didn't come. Instead she told him: 'You were wonderful. I didn't know you had it in you.' Leaning towards him his former controller gave him a warm kiss on the cheek. There were reasons however, that as well as being a real relief it could also create major problems.

He glanced across the way to where Hella was sitting alone in a doubt seat.

A single tear rolled gently down her cheek, even though she was doing her best to appear totally disinterested in the conversation.

But far from making the situation worse, Grace actually saved it.

'I'm sorry Robert,' she murmured. 'So sorry.'

'Sorry? What for?'

'I can't marry you.'

'I'm not surprised after what I've done.'

But Grace shook her head.

'It's not that. You really are a hero and I'm sorry. But there's someone else.'

'You bet there is!' Robert cried and then realised what he had said.

'Oh, I'm sorry again. You know I didn't mean it like that.'

But when his former fiancée burst out laughing instead of berating him the truth dawned at last.

'You,' he choked. 'You meant you had someone else!'

'Yes.'

'Who?'

Grace stopped laughing and he saw her features flood with love. She turned to the part-time eunuch sitting next to her, took hold of his hand and added: 'I should have thought you'd have guessed!'

But Robert wasn't listening any more. He was stumbling across to where his beautiful Hella was now sobbing openly – but full of joy – and falling into her waiting arms!

Game, set and match for all concerned.

THE END

Printed in Great Britain
by Amazon